THE HOSTAGE

THE HOSTAGE

A Novel by
Zayd Mutee' Dammaj

translated from the Arabic by
May Jayyusi and Christopher Tingley

with introductions by
Robert D. Burrowes
and
'Abd al-'Aziz al-Maqalih

preface by
Salma Khadra Jayyusi

INTERLINK BOOKS
An imprint of Interlink Publishing Group, Inc.
NEW YORK

First published in English 1994 by

INTERLINK BOOKS
An imprint of Interlink Publishing Group, Inc.
99 Seventh Avenue
Brooklyn, New York 11215

Originally published in Arabic as *Ar-Rahina*
by Dar al-Adab, Beirut, 1984

Library of Congress Cataloging-in-Publication Data

Dammaj, Zayd Mutee', 1943–
    [Rahinah, English]
    The hostage / by Zayd Mutee' Dammaj : translated from the
Arabic by May Jayyusi and Christopher Tingley.
        p.   cm. — (Emerging voices. New international fiction)
    ISBN 1–56656–146–9 — ISBN 1–56656–140–X (pbk.)
    I. Title.   II. Series.
  PJ7820.A513R3513 1994   94–2635
  892'. 736—dc20   CIP

Cover painting by Naziha Selim, courtesy of The Royal Society
of Fine Art, Jordan National Gallery of Fine Arts, Amman, Jordan.

Printed and bound in the United States of America

10 9 8 7 6 5 4 3 2 1

Acknowledgements

My deepest appreciation goes to the author, Zayd Mutee' Dammaj, for the ready help he gave us during the translation of his novel, explaining the various Yemeni terms unknown to us, and for the generous appreciation he has shown for the work. I must also warmly thank Dr. 'Abd al-'Aziz al-Maqalih, Rector of Sanaa University for finding time from his many responsibilities to write the introduction on the fictional background to *The Hostage*. Warm gratitude and scholarly acknowledgment go, too, to Dr. Robert Burrowes, Professor of History at the University of Washington and a specialist in the history of modern Yemen, who wrote the politico-historical introduction indispensable to the understanding of the novel's political basis. I must further thank the translators, May Jayyusi and Christopher Tingley, for their painstaking and affectionate work in rendering a delightful text which, for all its simple appearance, presented considerable technical difficulties of translation. Last but not least, I wish to thank the American Institute of Yemeni Studies (AIYS) for financial support provided to PROTA in the final stages of preparation.

Salma Khadra Jayyusi

This translation was prepared by PROTA, Project of Translation from Arabic Literature, founded and directed by Salma Khadra Jayyusi.

Other PROTA titles in print:

The Secret Life of Saeed, the Ill-Fated Pessoptimist, a novel by Emile Habiby. Trans. by S. K. Jayyusi and Trevor LeGassick. 1982; 2nd ed. 1985.

Wild Thorns, a novel by Sahar Khalifeh. Trans. by Trevor LeGassick and Elizabeth Fernea. 1985 and 1989.

Songs of Life, poetry by Abu 'l-Qasim al-Shabbi. Trans. by Lena Jayyusi and Naomi Shihab Nye. 1985.

War in the Land of Egypt, a novel by Yusuf al-Qa'id. Trans. by Olive Kenny and Christopher Tingley. 1986.

Modern Arabic Poetry: An Anthology. 1988 and 1991.

The Literature of Modern Arabia: An Anthology. 1987 and 1991.

All That's Left to You, a novella and collection of short stories by Ghassan Kanafani. Trans. by May Jayyusi and Jeremy Reed. 1990.

A Mountainous Journey, an autobiography by Fadwa Tuqan. Trans. by Olive Kenny. 1990.

The Sheltered Quarter, a novel by Hamza Bogary. Trans. by Olive Kenny and Jeremy Reed. 1991.

The Fan of Swords, poetry by Muhammad al-Maghut. Trans. by May Jayyusi and Naomi Shihab Nye. 1991.

A Balcony Over the Fakihani, a collection of three novellas by Liyana Badr. Trans. by Peter Clark with Christopher Tingley. 1993.

Prairies of Fever, a novel by Ibrahim Nasrallah. Trans. by May Jayyusi and Jeremy Reed. 1993.

Legacy of Muslim Spain. Essays on Islamic Civilization in the Iberian Peninsula. Ed. Salma Khadra Jayyusi. 1992.

Anthology of Modern Palestinian Literature. 1992.

Contents

Preface   viii
Introduction: Historical Background   1
Introduction: Literary Background   14

THE HOSTAGE   21

About the Translators   152

Preface

This novel was selected for translation, first, because it is a cogently written narrative serving the prerequisite of all fiction: the entertainment of the reader. It was also chosen, however, because it is highly informative, dealing as it does with unique experiences from a bygone age. Novels of this kind are extremely rich in information which would otherwise either be forgotten or remain buried in books of a scholarly nature which few readers tend to consult. Set in the form of a fictional narrative, and imbued with human experience and emotion, past events can be vibrantly restored to life, as this novel consummately demonstrates.

Zayd Mutee' Dammaj's *The Hostage* deals fundamentally with atrocity, with a world of exploitation within which the destiny of a human being seems totally in the hands of others; yet it is, at the same time, a work about freedom and individual salvation, showing how, for all the onslaught on a person's body and mind, a clear line of insight and sound judgment may be retained, reflecting an instinctive grasp of virtue and dignity.

Can a life shaped by atrocity, subjugated constantly to the will of others, lead to great and heroic acts? Heroic acts are magnanimous by nature and should rise above the impulse to vengeance. They should seek, at least in the expectations of the protagonist, to open up new avenues, to be a beginning for something greater than themselves. The protagonist of *The Hostage*, a youth from the countryside taken hostage by the ruling Imam's soldiers to ensure his father's and his clan's acquiescence, cannot openly challenge the authority that hems him in. In the context of the Imam's iron regime, the result of rebellious action would undoubtedly be the unobtrusive demise of the hostage himself. Direct heroism, therefore, is stifled, and, as such, *The Hostage* does not deal with great acts of courage and valor. What is needed here is endurance, the preservation of a defensive shield able to protect the protagonist against the loss of an inner freedom of spirit and moral discrimination which he will need later on, when he is finally free. Such endurance will necessarily entail polite behavior rather than bold challenge, although small acts of courage, as when the protagonist throws the insolent young prince into the pool, do in fact occur.

The experience of such a hostage, flung into the life of the palace with its pampered yet oppressed women, its authoritarian men, its soldiers and guards, is radically different from the simple experience of a country boy born to a family of courageous people who have rebelled against the Imam. Between the protagonist's feigned acquiescence and his instinctive inner rejection of atrocity and humiliation, a third element intervenes. For, besieged and cut off from family and familiar country traditions, he falls back on the remaining available resources of body and heart; hence his early sexual awakening and the moving friendships he forms.

In the foul atmosphere of palace life, he, like his friend the handsome *duwaydar* now dying of tuberculosis, is a focus for sexual exploitation on the part of the older palace women—women who are in almost the same position as the hostage himself, for they too are hemmed in, and through their exclusion from the normal experiences of life in a free society, suffer a similar deprivation which has led them to exploit the early virility of these young hostages, who are completely at their mercy. The protagonist is more fortunate than the handsome *duwaydar*, in that he attracts the desire of the beautiful young noblewoman, Sharifa Hafsa, with whom he has an intense though short-lived sexual experience.

In his description of these palace women—haughty, jealous and petty-minded—the author faithfully avoids arousing our sympathy with their victimized situation. The novel is, in fact, a crisp account of past decadence, and, except for the last chapter and those passages dealing with the suffering and death of the handsome *duwaydar*, is imbued not with a grim, sorrowful tone, but with an underlying irony which permeates the whole narrative. Such irony cannot, of course, entertain a generally sympathetic tone; yet Dammaj, as a true artist, makes a point of playing periodically on our sympathies, bringing sorrow abruptly to the surface by repeating the little song the guards would sing to the hostages:

Your mother, oh *duwaydar*, is distracted by her loss;
Her tears fall like rain . . .

The love of the mother for the child, which preserves its moving appeal in most cultures, retains a still greater store of emotional memory within Arabic culture.

Another diversion is the periodic inclusion of comic episodes. Every now and then, the wry, subtle and sophisticated ironic tone is interspersed with comic, sometimes even hilarious scenes; and by thus merging the comic with the ironic and the satirical, Dammaj mitigates the somber gravity of the theme, while continuing to emphasize the corrosive impact of decadence. Human degeneration under an evil regime is demonstrated not simply in its tragic toll on the innocence and vulnerability of the hostages, and on the young life of the dying handsome *duwaydar*, but in its comic aspects too, reflected in unforgettably humorous scenes of hypocrisy, pettiness and lust: the older palace women who, toothless or with rotting, yellow teeth, squabble over trivial matters or compete for the youthful prowess of the young hostages; the member of the palace staff engaged in bestiality (the hilarious mule episode); the subdued manner of the Governor who, driven by fear for his position, promptly cedes his son's car, the first and only car in Yemen, to the Crown Prince; and so on. Yet the images presented here also contain an element of the pathetic, often, indeed, verging on the tragic. Such grotesque behavior is, finally, people's reaction to a suffocating, regimented life under a hateful autocracy.

We are kept aware, in the background, of firm and courageous people who represent a constant threat to this rule; and it is awareness of such people and pride in their struggle that protects the protagonist against infection from the haughtiness, selfishness and corruption of the palace dwellers. This is a novel that speaks well of Yemen. There is something uniquely dignified in the Yemeni character, a quality which centuries of oppression have failed to touch, and which has perhaps been upheld by the enduring traditions of courage, sanctity of honor, and open-hearted hospitality which have characterized the best in Arabic culture from time immemorial.

No society, of course, operates without its wayward negative characters: the climbers, spongers, opportunists, spies, and fake propagandists who contrive a fat living for themselves by accommodating the needs of state or of powerful individuals. A good example of these is the court poet in this novel, who eulogizes the men in power in words betraying hypocrisy and affectation. This is not the place for a discussion of the panegyric in classical Arabic poetry, or of the major classical poets who eulogized great and powerful men, but we should note that, at the hands of such poets, eulogy was more than a means of achieving personal status and favor in high places. It was a tool which helped defend an empire, that empire's mouthpiece and its intellectual support, the prime means of asserting the power and greatness of the state; and it served to propagate great qualities in rulers and other men of status: generosity, magnanimity, honor and authority. Yet though the tradition has continued into modern times (in both poetry and prose, and notably in journalism), it has now come to smack of the hypocritical and the derivative. However, if a number of scenes in the novel betray an obsequious attitude toward those in higher positions, such scenes involve only those whose lives are dependent on officialdom. The protagonist and his friend, though completely at the mercy of their jailors, are never servile or unduly humble.

For, even in an age of atrocity, a resistant fiber holds the constant possibility of deliverance; and such high spirit is seen not only in the resistance of a community far removed from the place of action of the novel, but also within the individual protagonist battling alone against the odds of his fate, as he remains besieged within the sealed world of the palace. The communal resistance in Aden, where the Free People's Party was preparing for liberation, has no links whatever with those individual prisoners, who, for all their forced acquiescence to the life imposed upon them, remain free at heart. This makes *The Hostage* very different from other political novels in contemporary Arabic literature. The Palestinian novel (to take a single example, Liyana Badr's recent novel, *Eye of the Mirror*) almost always reflects the spirit of the community: the way Palestinians support one another in their personal tragedies turns each such tragedy into a communal experience of the most poignant kind, holding the people together and affording them the hope of survival—for though the individual dies, sometimes even ending a family line, he or she nevertheless extends the possibility of life for the dispersed nation. The heroic defiance of the individual here dons greater significance, cementing the communal will to struggle on and never to yield. In *The Hostage*, by contrast, the death of the handsome *duwaydar* is heartbreaking because it is so gratuitous, because it is denied the allure and pride of martyrdom for country and honor. Lying in complete obscurity in a humble corner of the Governor's palace, the dying *duwaydar* spends his last moments of life agonizing over the unresolved outcome of a revolution that will eventually avenge his plight without ever having heard of him.

In writing this novel, Dammaj seems resolved to etch the memory of such hostages on the mind of his contemporaries, and on that of the world. The successful young revolution, however much it strives, through the various channels of information and a widely diffused delineation of pre-revolutionary atrocities, to convince the world of its justice, can never really dramatize past experiences as this novel does. This is the secret of fiction: its enduring capacity to bring human experience back to life in its minutest details, dramatically resurrecting history from the realm of oblivion.

The novel's open-ended final scene anticipates the coming of a radical, unforeseeable change which the author, rightly, does not define. The spectacle of the youth running away from the cemetery where he has just laid to rest the body of his friend, away from the place which has robbed him of his innocence, away from the young woman for whom he cares but whose aristocratic culture he loathes, toward an open future that can only promise freedom, demonstrates the impossibility of ending the novel with a precise conclusion. Yet, it closes, too, on a highly symbolic, highly dramatic note. Following the burial, a whole world of freedom opens up for the young fleeing hostage; and through the sorrow that hovers over the cemetery, a new hope surges up.

Such open-endedness also saves the novel from ideology; and this is one of its strongest points. The whole issue of oppression and suffering is transformed into personal experience, into an individual knowledge of their dimensions which transcends ideological and communal struggle, plunging into the realm of human suffering which the protagonist, like all of us, can only experience alone.

Salma Khadra Jayyusi
Director, PROTA (Project
of Translation from Arabic)

Introduction: Historical Background

*Robert D. Burrowes**

Z ayd Mutee' Dammaj's novel *The Hostage* is set in the highlands of Yemen during the late 1940s, towards the end of the time of the Imams and the beginning of the republican era. The novel revolves around the lives of some of the young boys the Imam regularly took from their families as hostages in order to secure the obedience of their fathers, tribes, or villages; the boys lived together, often in harsh circumstances, often separated from family and childhood friends for many years. The novel about these boys is about darkness and light, the darkness of being hostage to the past and tradition as well as to the

* Robert D. Burrowes is a writer and consultant on Middle East politics as well as an adjunct professor at the Henry M. Jackson School of International Studies at the University of Washington. He is the author of *The Yemen Arab Republic: The Politics of Development, 1962–1986* (1987) and *Yemen: An Historical Dictionary* (1993).

1

Imam, and the light of the struggle for freedom and change. It is about being born in a place that is a remnant of the remote past, the growing awareness of its "backwardness," and the fight against this condition.

North Yemen, officially the Yemen Arab Republic (YAR), was located on the margins of the Arab world, on the southwest corner of the Arabian Peninsula, the corner that is bounded by the Red Sea and the Gulf of Aden. It shared this corner of Arabia with South Yemen, or the People's Democratic Republic of Yemen (PDRY). These two Yemeni states ceased to exist when they merged to form the Republic of Yemen in 1990. However, before the creation of the YAR and the PDRY in the 1960s there was traditional North Yemen and the Yemeni Imamate, as well as the British colonial presence in South Yemen.

Modernity came late to North Yemen. On the eve of the 1962 revolution, North Yemen was one of the world's last extant examples of a relatively complex, large-scale traditional social system. A highly tribalized and conservative Islamic society, it was little changed in the 1950s from the Yemen of two or even several centuries earlier. Perhaps most like the Afghanistan of about 1900, it was virtually devoid of piped water, surfaced roads, motor vehicles and engines, electricity, telephones or radios—much less the modern ideas and institutions that go with these things. North Yemen, at the dawn of the Space Age, was in, but not of, the twentieth century.

Centered in the interior highlands, traditional Yemen persisted in part because it was geographically isolated from a rapidly changing world by a hot, malaria-ridden coastal desert backed by high, rugged mountains enshrouded in dense haze. Despite the nearness of Britain's bustling Aden Colony and modern commerce's major sea lane between Europe and Asia, North Yemen remained a backwater, outside the mainstream of world events during the last decades of the age of imperialism; it was, as one diplomat put it, "the Tibet of the Red Sea."

The oil fever of the middle third of the twentieth century, which fixed attention on the other side of the Arabian Peninsula, served to reinforce this situation. Moreover, Yemen's traditional economy, based upon subsistence agriculture and human and animal energy, was to a remarkable degree self-contained and self-sufficient. Although life was austere for most and severe deprivation quite common, the Yemenis produced nearly all of what they consumed; the few luxury and essential products that they imported were paid for by the export of small amounts of coffee, cotton, and animal hides and skins. In sum, North Yemen and the modern world had little economic need for or interest in each other, and traditional Yemen remained intact partly for this reason.

To a considerable degree, however, traditional Yemen persisted by design. Noting that North Yemen had undergone some modernization during the second Ottoman Turkish occupation that ended with World War I, the scholar Robin Bidwell observed that "the fact that the Sanaa of the 1950s seemed a museum was not the result of centuries of neglect but of a conscious decision by . . . [two Imams] to hold the twentieth century at bay." In an era when the world's few remaining traditional societies were crumbling under the impact of modernity, these two remarkable men revived and reinvigorated traditional Yemen at the same time as they insulated it almost completely from the outside world. Imam Yahya (1869–

3

1948), who in 1904 became the second member of the Hamid al-Din family to occupy the Imamate, strove to contain the new ideas and practices that had entered Yemen with the Ottomans. He and his son and successor, Imam Ahmad (c.1891–1962), were also able to limit the impact on Yemen of the rising tide of modernism and nationalism that engulfed the Arab world in the four decades after World War I. Between them, Yahya and Ahmad occupied the imamate and guarded Yemen's ramparts from 1904 until 1962, allowing as few Yemenis as possible to leave the country and even fewer outsiders to enter Yemen with their alien ideas and artifacts.

Imam Yahya's inwardness is apparent in the fact that he never set foot outside the country or even laid eyes on the Red Sea, which lies only thirty miles from the foot of the highlands whereon he resided. A xenophobe, Yemen's "old man of the mountain" knew enough about the outside world—and of the encounters of western imperialism with India, China, and the Ottoman Empire—not to want to have much to do with it. Allegedly, he once said that he would rather eat straw than risk foreign ties that could cost Yemen its independence.

The Yemeni imamate was the political expression of Zaydism, the branch of Shii Islam to which most of the people of the northern half of North Yemen adhere. Founded in the tenth century C.E., the Zaydi imamate existed more or less continuously into the twentieth century, sometimes strong and often weak, sometimes unoccupied or claimed by rival contestants. The imamate fit comfortably into sociologist Max Weber's category of "patrimonial traditional political system," in that it was sacred—or theocratic—and operated largely within limits set and justified by custom and tradition. According to Zaydi political thought, the Imam was the secular and religious leader of the community of the faithful and was elected by the *ulama*—those learned in religion—and other Zaydi notables. He could be elected only from those males who had, among many other attributes, direct descent from the Prophet Muhammad via Fatima and Ali. The imamate was theoretically nonhereditary and open to all Zaydis who possessed the required attributes. In practice, it tended toward dynastic rule, the Hamid al-Din family being but the latest of the several great Zaydi families that have occupied this position over recent centuries.

Zaydi doctrine made the welfare and protection— moral as well as physical—of the community of believers the primary duty of the Imam; by all accounts, both Yahya and Ahmad were devout men who took this charge seriously. As Harold Ingrams, a colonial officer with years of service in the Aden Protectorate, said: "The Imam's rule *is* stern, and he keeps peace by methods which we should not like, but only a small percentage actually suffer out of a population of several million. The taxation (and extortion) are heavy, but certainly not so heavy that it is uneconomic to labour."

Imam Yahya would not have been able to isolate and revitalize traditional Yemen as much as he did had he not strengthened the imamate and extended its sway during the three decades after the final withdrawal of the Ottomans in 1918. Due to his leadership in the struggle against the hated Turks, the legitimacy of the imamate and its occupant was enhanced and a sense of national identity was reinforced, at least among the Zaydis of the northern highlands. Imam Yahya and his several princely sons, Ahmad among them, established firm Zaydi rule of the southern uplands and the arid coast, areas populated by Sunni Muslims of the Shafii school who felt no religious allegiance to the Zaydi imamate. They garrisoned these areas with troops from the highlands and even "colonized" them with Zaydis, both prominent families and minor functionaries. In consolidating and extending the imamate, the Hamid al-Din family also tipped the millennium-old balance of power between the state and the tribes—between the center and the periphery—in favor of the former. Most of the tribes in the north and east, as well as those down near the coast, chose or were compelled to offer at least nominal allegiance to the Imam. As a result, the geographic limits of North Yemen in modern times were reached in the mid-1930s.

Under Yahya and Ahmad, the imamate was truly the Imam's government, one over which he exercised direct personal control. Hugh Scott, who had audiences with Imam Yahya in the late 1930s, said it best: "He is as absolute a monarch as any left in the world. No ruler can in greater measure attend personally to every detail of his administration—as we had opportunity to see with our own eyes. . . . If anyone on earth can say 'I am the State,' it is the Imam of Yemen." Virtually no distinction was made, in theory or practice, between the Imam's household and the imamate and its treasury. The highest officials were usually personal confidants of the Imam and often members of his household; indeed, most top positions in the 1930s and 1940s were held by Yahya's several older sons. High officials were also drawn from prominent families claiming descent from the Prophet and from the great juristic families known for their mastery of Islamic law and theology. Below these top people, in addition to a corps of lowly clerks and scribes, there was a small, somewhat specialized and differentiated official-dom charged with collecting taxes, settling disputes, and carrying out other routine affairs of state.

Clearly, the imamate state that Yahya and Ahmad ruled so absolutely did not amount to much by modern standards. It was neither extensive or intensive in its reach, lacked all ministerial structure, and was only slightly differentiated structurally from the rest of society. As a result, the capacity of the Imam to penetrate his society, to regulate behavior in it, to draw resources from it, and to use those resources as he saw fit was quite limited. The constraints on the imamate are perhaps best seen in its relationship to the two major tribal confederations in Yemen's north and east. Since their standing army was small, ill-equipped, and for the most part poorly trained, the Imams for centuries had been forced to depend on these confederations—the "wings of the imamate," as they were called—for subsidized tribal irregulars. The paramount shaykhs gave this support and provided defense in exchange for a great measure of local autonomy, the result being that the tribes were less the loyal subjects than the sometime allies of the Imams.

Although the ragtag army and bureaucracy was improved somewhat by Imam Yahya with leftover Ottoman organization, procedures, and personnel, the enhanced strength of the imamate during the four decades after World War I was primarily the result of the forceful personalities, dedication, energy, and hard work of Yahya and Ahmad. Skilled practitioners of traditional politics, they used military campaigns, the hostage system, gifts and subsidies, factional manipulation, and other arcane devices both to consolidate their power vis-a-vis challengers at the center and to extend their sway slightly on the periphery at the expense of local notables and the tribes. They achieved these results largely within the limits of traditional practice and without the help of the ideas and techniques of modern statecraft. As late as the end of the 1950s, perhaps the most important modern tool of the imamate was the telegraph, a legacy of Ottoman times which the Imams controlled directly and used to check personally on tax receipts and political conditions in the major towns.

The game of politics in imamate Yemen was the preserve of a tiny minority at the top of a largely closed system; it was based on loose, shifting cliques and factions, and was conducted on a personal, face-to-face basis. The major actors were members of the ruling family, the heads of the other great families, leading *ulama* and jurists, and tribal shaykhs. By contrast, most of the people—tribespeople and peasants as well as artisans, shopkeepers, and merchants—rarely if ever had any political relevance or role to play. The Imam maintained direct contact with his subjects through daily sessions of his *diwan*, audiences to which the lowliest petitioner theoretically had access. Officials and secret informers served as the eyes and ears of the Imam, keeping him in touch with the society beyond the palace and *diwan*. The flow of demands and supports into the political system was not handled by specialized political structures such as organized interest groups or political parties, but rather by government officials, local notables, or family heads at all levels of Yemeni society. The absence of such things as parties, pressure groups, and the mass media—the absence of any real need for a differentiated political infrastructure—was a major distinction between the imamate system of traditional Yemen and the more modern political systems growing up in Aden and in much of the rest of the Arab world in the first half of the twentieth century.

There were, however, breaches in the ramparts thrown up by the Imams to protect traditional Yemen from the corrupting influences of the modern world. The biggest breach was Britain's bustling, fast-growing Aden Colony, one of the world's busiest ports by the 1950s and the main entrepot for North Yemen's limited transactions with the outside world. Especially after World War II, a growing number of Yemenis, mostly Shafiis seeking escape from the poverty and limited opportunities at home, went south to Aden, first for work and later for education. Indeed, most of the port workers and other laborers in Aden were migrants from the north, as were many of the small shopkeepers and importers. A considerable number of North Yemenis also went abroad from Aden as sailors or to become merchants and laborers in Djibouti, Ethiopia, the Sudan, and as far away as Marseilles, Cardiff, Manchester, Brooklyn, Detroit, and California. More importantly, beginning in the 1940s, an increasing number of young Yemenis got the start of a modern education in Aden, and some of them went on for secondary and higher education in Cairo, other cities of the Arab world, and even Europe and the United States. Aden, called "the eye of Yemen" in Arabic literature, had by the 1950s become the window on and the door to the modern world for a tightly shuttered Yemen. Just outside the Imams' reach, this opening could not be closed down by them.

A second breach in the ramparts, one that did not assume much importance until after the 1940s, was caused by the seductive idea that tradition could be defended by the selective use of modern means. Unlike many rulers before and during his time, Imam Yahya had strongly resisted this idea. Nevertheless, he did send about a dozen young men to Iraq for training for about a year in 1936 and, more importantly, he allowed forty boys—later called the Famous Forty—to leave in 1947 for schooling first in Lebanon and then in Egypt and the West. The Famous Forty and a small number of cohorts made up the initial wave of educational emigrants from North Yemen, and many of them are still playing key roles in Yemen's development well over a generation after they first went abroad. In the 1950s, Imam Ahmad, though no modernizing traditionalist in the mold of the rulers of Iran or Afghanistan earlier in the century, succumbed to the temptations of outside ties and aid to a greater degree than had his father. Concerned by increased British activity in the Aden Protectorate and by the growing appeal of Gamal Abdel Nasser's brand of Arab nationalism, he looked abroad for political and military help. New strategic links with Nasser's Egypt led in the mid-1950s to an influx of Soviet arms and, more importantly, Egyptian military advisers. Economic aid agreements were also pursued, and in the early 1960s the Soviet Union was constructing a modern port and the Chinese and Americans were building North Yemen's first two modern highways. Imam Ahmad also allowed at least two more groups of students to go abroad, including a few members of the royal family, and, more importantly, was unable to prevent many others in search of education from slipping over the border to Aden and on to Egypt and elsewhere. Indeed, by 1960 the trickle of educational emigrants had swelled into a torrent, the number of secondary and university students abroad doubling between 1958 and 1961, reaching well over a thousand.

The beginning of modern politics came to North Yemen in the 1940s with the growing awareness of the "backwardness" of Yemen and the belief that the chief culprit was the imamate. The first major opposition group, the Free Yemenis, was founded in 1944, although it was preceded by a few years by two small clandestine groups. The Free Yemenis played a role in the failed attempt to oust the Hamid al-Din family on the occasion of the assassination of Imam Yahya in 1948. Although in existence for only a few years, the Free Yemenis led directly to the formation of other opposition groups in the 1950s, most notably the Yemeni Unionists. The propagandizing and other activities of these groups, clandestine within Yemen and open abroad, helped to create a climate that fostered plots and other acts against Imam Ahmad, including the failed 1955 coup attempt.

Far from being radical modernists, the Free Yemenis and other early dissidents were the mid-twentieth-century equivalents of the Turkish reformers of the Ottoman Empire during the Tanzimat period in the mid-nineteenth century. They evolved only slowly from favoring a constitutional imamate to favoring a republic, and their conception of republicanism was sketchy and a bit quaint. By the early 1950s, however, many of the still

11

small number of young Yemenis studying abroad and a few of the larger number working abroad had been drawn to other more modern and radical political groups. Many of these Yemenis were introduced to modern politics by way of the culturally congenial Muslim Brotherhood. Although a few stayed with the brotherhood, most of them migrated from it to secular political movements. Nurtured in Aden and the major political centers of the Arab world, Yemeni branches of the Communist Party and such pan-Arab entities as the Arab Nationalist Movement and the Baath party were founded and began to attract a Yemeni following. More importantly, by the mid-1950s a large number of Yemenis had been profoundly influenced by the Egyptian revolution of 1952 and came under the spell of Nasser and his evolving brand of nationalism and socialism. It was a heady time in the Arab world, and young Yemenis abroad sampled widely and became intoxicated by the varied forms of modern Arab politics.

The Yemen Arab Republic was created after a coup by young army officers on September 26, 1962, a week after Imam Ahmad died suddenly. Abolished forthwith were the imamate and, as important, the birthright of descendents of the Prophet to rule North Yemen. The joy and exuberant freedom of the first days of the republican era soon gave way to a wrenching decade, one marked by a long civil war and foreign intervention, great economic privation and social upheaval, and—above all—the rapid and irreversible opening of an unprepared North Yemen to the modern world. Between 1970 and 1990, the YAR and its Yemeni neighbor to the south, the PDRY, fitfully underwent a real measure of political development and socioeconomic modernization. In 1990, the two Yemeni states united, beginning a new, more promising era for Yemen and the Yemeni people.

Introduction: Literary Background

*'Abd al-'Aziz al-Maqalih**

It is somewhat difficult to speak of the short story or novel in a particular Arab country without also speaking of literary production in the context of the Arab world as a whole, particularly in those countries once regarded as the center of Arabic literature, i.e., Egypt and the countries comprising Greater Syria (Lebanon, Syria, Jordan and Palestine), where these modern literary genres first appeared and where they were considerably developed before subsequently taking root, in one country after another, on the periphery of the region. Among such countries are those that might be described as marginal or

---

* 'Abd al-'Aziz al-Maqalih is a Yemeni poet, writer, critic and scholar. He is the Rector of Sanaa University and of the Center for Yemeni Studies. His many collections of poetry include *Ma'rib Speaks*, *A Letter to Sayf ibn Dhi Yazan*, and *The Return of Waddah al-Yaman*.

forgotten regions, and of these Yemen is the most prominent example; for Yemen was, over the first half of this
century, sunk in a profound sleep by virtue of its total
underdevelopment, and because of occupation (British)
in the south, and tyranny (on the part of the Imams) in the
north.

While a full account of the genesis of the short story
and novel in Yemen will indeed reveal some anticipatory
short fiction, and even novelistic attempts, prior to the
revolution of October 14, 1962, these beginnings require
no more than fleeting mention; it is sufficient to note that
the real emergence of these genres awaited the stormy
changes sweeping through the country, from the north
down to the farthest southern regions, in the course of
this revolution. The country, both north and south, had
been grossly bereft of both knowledge and progress—had
become the prototype, indeed, of a place closed in on
itself, ignoring all calls for change. The situation of the
Yemeni creative writer was an unhappy one, especially in
the north, which was characterized by an overwhelmingly
rigid political system, of the utmost cruelty and harshness.
As such, authors had no opportunity to hone their techniques in the new fictional arts (which also included
theater) until the September–October Revolution de-
cisively opened the way for Yemen to enter the world
anew, affording Yemeni writers the right to entertain
change and the means to assimilate the new trends of
contemporary literary life, and so help them catch up with
other Arab writers who had already gone much further in
this field. It is not strange, therefore, that Yemeni writers,
within the various literary genres, should have emerged
from amongst Yemenis studying abroad, in Egypt and

other Arab and non-Arab countries. The short story following modern criteria was initially pioneered by Muhammad 'Abd al-Wali, and by Zayd Mutee' Dammaj; the latter was a student at the Tanta high school in Egypt when he made his first attempts at the short story in the early sixties. When he eventually returned to Sanaa at the end of the sixties he found that, while the revolution had endeavored to create a new reality in Yemen, freeing the country from chaos and corruption, this reality had in fact become full of contradictions, reflected, notably, in the presence of two opposing political orders within the same people and the same country, and in the disasters that had ensued from this bitter conflict, at all levels—political, social, intellectual and literary.

Dammaj, a writer who belonged to the Yemeni nation as a whole, could not maintain a neutral attitude in the face of such contradictions; and he began, through the vehicle of the short story, first to warn his people, then to criticize and exhort them. Anyone re-reading today, following the unification of Yemen, the immense treasury of short stories produced by Dammaj over a quarter of a century, will come to understand the depth of the relationship between this writer and his fictional world.

The Hostage, the splendid work to which I shall now turn, is the only novelistic work Dammaj has attempted, but it is also the work that has brought him considerable fame outside the Arab world, following its translation first into French and now into English. The work is, in fact, an urgent cry of protest, an attempt to depict the gross contradictions which were prevalent in the years before the revolution, and which provided the country with an inexhaustible source of literary material.

Yet, if it is *The Hostage* that has brought Dammaj major literary fame, his short story collections—*Tahish al-Huban* (1973); *Al-'Aqrab* (*The Scorpion*) (1982); *Al-Jisr* (*The Bridge*) (1986); and *Ahzan al-bint Mayyasa* (*The Sorrows of the Girl Mayyasa*) (1990)—have also established him imperishably as a major figure among writers of the short story in Yemen.

In Dammaj's novel, and also in his short stories, local characteristics are powerfully presented, achieving universality through the writer's ability to capture them spontaneously and simply. Other critics, besides myself, have noted Dammaj's considerable success in this connection; the way he is able, without obtrusiveness or affectation, to distill the major characteristics of particular local elements. His stories become, therefore, like pictures which not only reflect the life around him, but also depict a specific time, space and milieu, making readers, wherever they come from, feel they are reading the work of a story writer from Yemen and from no other Arab country. When writing a story, Dammaj preserved his own particular language; he was not attracted by any modernizing aim to invent a new language for the story through distinctive formal creations—although the new realism characterizing his work shows that he has in fact benefited from the general climate of change affecting literary creation in the Arab world.

It is relevant to note here that some of Dammaj's short stories are actually the nucleus of a longer work, but have never been developed into full-length novels. It is fortunate that the present work did have the opportunity to be developed at the hands of its creator, so providing a text which has become one of the most important novels yet to appear in Yemen. *The Hostage* has, happily, appeared in three editions in the Arab world itself, before subsequently appearing first in a French edition and now in this elegant English translation.

If it is true, as has been said, that the historical novel makes a people live its history anew, then *The Hostage*, which is in some degree a historical novel, has succeeded, for all its fictional character, in inducing the reader to grasp the most important aspects of the life of a decade—Yemen in the forties—which is still close to us today, a decade rich in specific local events that reflect attempts to lay foundations within a context of turbulent change, and so bring to an end the stagnation and rigidity of the region as a whole. During the forties, the radio had entered the homes of no one except the ruling elite, and the only car in the country traveled the road between the Governor's house and the Imam's palace. Any surviving beneficiaries of the old regime who care to read this novel should recognize that the novelist has not only been fair, but has in fact contrived, in his choice of characters and in his delineation of specific detail, to present the old state of affairs as less horrific and less repressive than it actually was.

Since *The Hostage* was published, people have constantly wondered whether the writer was describing his own experience or that of a fictional character. The truth is that Zayd Mutee' Dammaj was never taken hostage himself: he was the only son of his parents, and, within a family which was a focus of the regime's fears and anxieties, the harsh role of "hostage" was indeed the fate of a number of his relatives and childhood companions, but Dammaj himself was spared. I would not, however, think it impossible that the events of the story represent a re-living of some other person's past experiences, arousing a particular reaction, and feeding a residual obsession within the writer himself. Certainly his other words are not free of ambiguous reminiscences of a childhood world filled with lingering memories and sorrows.

THE HOSTAGE

How beautiful this city was!
I'd seen it first when I was taken from my village and imprisoned in the fortress of al-Qahira as one of the hostages of the Imam. His soldiers had come, in their blue uniforms, and torn me from my mother's lap and the arms of the rest of my family; then, not content with that, they'd seized my father's horse too, in accordance with the Imam's wishes.

It was a fine day. The fierce rains had slackened and the sky was clear, so that we could see the city, and the distant villages sparkling on the mountaintops. It was the month of *Allan*, when people were getting ready for the harvest.

I was up on the lofty roof of the Governor's palace with

23

my companion, the *duwaydar*,[1] the "handsome *duwaydar*," as everyone called him. Why I so cherished his friendship I don't know. Perhaps it was because we were about the same age, or because we did the same kind of work together.

It was only recently that I'd been taken from the al-Qahira fortress and brought here to the residence of the Governor, who ruled over the city and the surrounding countryside as the Imam's representative. As I was led through the gates of the palace, I could still see in my mind the looks of disdain with which the other hostages in the fortress had taken their leave of me.

I knew that some hostages had, in the past, been taken off to the palaces of the Imam, or those of his princes and governors, to serve as their *duwadera*. Some of them, I heard, had managed to escape; others had tried and failed, and had then been brought back to the fortress and put in chains there for the rest of their lives.

What I couldn't grasp was exactly what a *duwaydar* was, and what sort of work he was supposed to do. Perhaps I was too young to understand the explanations I was given. A *duwaydar* was, among other things, a boy who hadn't yet reached the age of puberty. So much I gathered from the *faqih*[2] who was our fellow-prisoner, and who was given the job of instructing us in the Qur'an and in our duties as obedient prisoners at the fortress. Also, the *faqih* would tell us, such boys now did the work once done by the *tawashiyeh*, or eunuchs, explaining, as we looked puzzled,

---

[1] *Duwaydar*: A smart young boy employed by princes and governors in their palaces. The plural is *duwadera*.
[2] *Faqih*: A religious teacher.

that these were castrated slaves. As our puzzlement then increased, he'd explain matters further: they were slaves whose testicles had been removed. Still our bewilderment would deepen at the mention of this cruel act, and he'd add that this was done so that the slaves wouldn't indulge in shameful acts of the sexual sort, like sleeping with the women of the palace; in other words, they'd lose their manhood and become impotent. Finally, as we showed no signs of grasping what he was saying, he'd shout angrily:

"That's enough now! Don't you understand?"

"No, Sir," we'd answer, "we don't."

He'd fly into a furious temper at this, regarding our reply as insolence. And we'd respond with our usual refrain:

"May God forgive you, Sir ... and may He forgive your parents ... and our parents ..."

*   *   *

Some hostages who'd served as *duwadera*, and then returned to the fortress on "attaining puberty" (as the *faqih* called it), had the most amazing tales to tell. The features of most of them had, I noticed, changed. Their faces were pale now, while their bodies, on the other hand, had taken on a general smoothness of texture, and showed signs of premature flabbiness and weakness. I'd noticed, too, the interest they aroused in the fortress guards because of their smooth skins and soft voices, and their spotless clothes hanging down to the floor, and their embroidered kerchiefs, woven for them by the women of the palace, which they wore on their heads to hide their carefully combed, curly hair. From this hair would arise the scent of perfumed oils, which the guards would breathe in with evident pleasure. So, too, would our teacher, the *faqih*, who treated them with an exaggerated and rather silly show of consideration; and when some of us complained at this partial treatment, he'd lose his temper.

"Be quiet, you riffraff!" he'd shout. "You animals! God save us all from your sort!"

"May God forgive you, Sir," we'd reply. "And may He forgive your parents . . . and our parents . . . Oh, God, the Compassionate, the Benefactor . . ."

When the class was over, we hostages would go and sit on top of the walls overlooking the city, swinging our legs in the air and looking out towards the distant horizon, each one searching for his village beyond the mountains.

Although our *faqih* always had a stick in his hand, he never dared raise it against us. Only once had he ever hit one of the hostages with it, and he'd had his arm broken and his beard plucked out as a result. He never tried it again.

*   *   *

When I arrived at the Governor's house, my new friend the *duwaydar* greeted me with a warmth which quite took me aback, and he began to show me round every part of the great palace, and all its surrounding buildings. We'd encounter women of different ages, and varying, too, in their beauty, and neatness, and the attractiveness of their dress. He'd introduce me to them, and each time I'd hold myself aloof.

"This is the Governor's aunt . . ."

"This is the Governor's sister . . . the divorced one . . ."

"This is the Governor's daughter . . ."

"This is the Governor's second wife . . ."

"This is his first wife . . ."

"This is the new servant girl . . . she's really beautiful, isn't she? . . ."

"This is the old one . . ."

"This one milks the cows . . ."

"This is the governess . . . the governess to the children and . . ."

I made no answer to any of this. I'd shrink back if they patted me on the shoulder, and recoil if one of them stretched out her hand to pinch my cheek or playfully rub my lips—it filled me with disgust. And all the while my friend was grinning from ear to ear as he rushed me down wide staircases, inlaid with square stones, and on to the Turkish baths.

These consisted of a vault, with cupolas above and corridors leading off it, all inlaid with square black stones, held together by a cement made from white lime. A dense steam rose towards marble-framed windows through which the light gleamed. I stood hesitantly at the entrance.

"Don't worry!" my companion said. "It isn't the women's day!"

"Men's day or women's day, I'm not coming in here again."

"Do you know something? You and I are the only people in this palace who are allowed to come in here at any time—whether it's the women's day or the men's day!"

I shuddered.

"I shan't ever be coming in here," I said.

"Oh, you will," he said, pulling me off towards the deserted stables.

He started telling me stories about the things he'd seen in the baths, and about the women—the young ones, and the old ones, and, especially, the unmarried ones among them, and how overjoyed they always were when he went to serve them.

*   *   *

The stables were large, and from them came a smell that reminded me of the lower part of our house in the mountains—a smell of droppings and cow's urine mixed with hay and fodder, all mingled with the clucking of chickens disturbed by our arrival as they foraged for insects in the dunghills. I remembered how careful my father had always been to keep brass bells fastened round the necks of the bulls. Whenever I went through the lower part of our house, or to the spring, or to the meadows, their music would fill me with delight. On our mountain-side even the camels and donkeys had these old brass bells hung round their necks, so as to warn people, especially children, who might be coming along the roads and tracks.

To my astonishment, all I saw through the whole length and breadth of the Governor's stables was a couple of mules (his milking cows were in a separate place near the back entrance to the palace).

My companion the *duwaydar* enlightened me.

"The Imam and his heir, the Crown Prince Sayf al-Islam, have the horses taken to their own palaces. All they leave behind is a few mules and donkeys."

28

"I can't see any donkeys at all."

"We're the donkeys—the two of us and the rest!"

He meant it as a harmless joke, but I didn't find it amusing. As we reached the gates of the stable, and stood facing the spacious courtyard, I realized the place was not just one palace, but many palaces, some of them old and some new.

"That old brick building," my companion said, "is reserved for the Governor's pampered divorced sister. She's a beautiful woman."

"You mean all that's hers?"

"She's from a different mother, and the mother left her a bigger fortune than the Governor was left by his father."

I was too busy looking round to ask any further questions.

"Her name's Hafsa," he went on. "Sharifa Hafsa."[3]

I listened attentively. He paused to suppress a deep sigh, then went on.

"In the end she managed to force her cousin to divorce her. Then," he continued, seeing my interest, "there was a big crisis, and our Master the Crown Prince intervened on her side."

I didn't answer; and, before I could ask about the reason for the divorce, he added, by way of explanation:

"Her marriage to her cousin was to the Governor's advantage."

I shrugged my shoulders to show I didn't follow.

"The Governor's married to her cousin's sister," he said—I smiled at the paradoxical riddle behind his

---

[3] Sharifa: A title applied to a woman of noble birth, claiming descent from the Prophet.

words—"and the marriage was arranged to stop the inheritance going elsewhere. This way there'd be an equal inheritance. But she rejected her cousin from the very first night—he used to chew *qat*[4] from nightfall till dawn."

"Was that the reason for the divorce?" I broke in.

He smiled with pleasure at my active interest in what he was saying.

"It wasn't just that," he said. "There were other pressing reasons too. For one thing he was so old and feeble he couldn't have relations with her. He already had a lot of wives, and countless children."

None of this surprised me in the least, and I felt no need to inquire further; but I continued to listen with attention as we walked towards the house.

"She's young," he said, "the youngest one of the family, and her father used to love her and pamper her because of his love for her mother—she was the youngest of his wives, and the richest and most beautiful as well."

I didn't feel in the least tired that day, even though I'd wandered with my friend through most parts of his amazing world. He, for his part, was happy and full of gaiety, overjoyed that I was there and concentrating all his attention on me. People kept on calling out to him, and he took not the slightest notice of them!

His room was at a turning of one of the broad staircases.

"This is our room," he said, drawing me inside.

"Our room?"

"Yes."

He left abruptly, and I went to the single small window

---

[4] *Qat*: A plant with green leaves chewed as a narcotic in Yemen.

and squatted there, studying the room at my leisure. There was a small mattress with a lot of holes in it through which the straw stuffing peered out, and a black half-woollen blanket folded at the top of the bed, over a grubby pillow whose cotton cover he was evidently too lazy to wash.

To one side was a cheaply dyed wooden chest, which he'd placed next to the worn-out mattress to stop it sliding while he was asleep, and to make it easier for him to open it whenever he wanted to. This chest held his clothes and other possessions.

My gaze moved on to some pictures he'd stuck on the wall—I wasn't quite sure how he'd managed to make them stay there, but I suspected he might just have used his spittle. There were pictures of a succession of beautiful golden-haired girls with blue eyes, a kind of girl I'd never seen before; he told me later that he'd cut them out from papers and magazines which were sent to the Governor from foreign countries. There were also some pictures of people in strange clothes.

"This is the Führer," he'd say, in the tones of a learned lecturer, "Hitler, that is. And this is Mussolini, the king of the Italians. And this venerable *shaykh*[5] here is al-Mukhtar . . . Omar al-Mukhtar."[6]

He was proud of knowing so many things I didn't, and his air of superiority would grow still more pronounced as he talked about listening to the international news on the Governor's radio, and about how he was the only one who could make the set work as a great crowd of people

---

[5] *Shaykh*: An old man, or a title of dignity given to men of high breeding or great learning; it also means a teacher or a man who performs clerical duties.

[6] Omar al-Mukhtar: A famous Libyan revolutionary, who led the revolt against the Italians and was subsequently executed.

gathered round it, both inside the palace and outside. He knew all the stations and programs and signals. "Now," he'd say, laughing to make fun of me, "we'll hear Big Ben striking, which means that it's four p.m. Greenwich Mean Time . . . Now it's time for Yunis Bahri's[7] commentary from Radio Berlin." And I'd laugh too, struck with wonder at all these things which were so new to me.

He brought me a mattress and blanket, and, before laying them down on the ground, asked me which corner of the room I'd like.

"It's for the host to decide where the guest goes," I said jokingly.

He laughed, threw the mattress and blanket down in the corner opposite his, then sat down next to me and started talking again.

"I don't suppose you know what a gramophone is, do you?" he said.

I turned down my mouth, to show my puzzlement at his words.

"It's just a machine," he said, "bigger than a radio, which sends out beautiful songs, of people like al-Qutabi and al-Awtari al-Mas and Shaykh Ali Abu Bakr."[8]

He gave the names of some further people I'd perhaps just heard of, though I'd never heard them sing, and he mentioned other names too, which I later learned were those of other singers from the Arab World.

He dragged me off there and then to a marvelous corner of the palace which was gorgeously furnished and spotlessly clean. There he sat me down on a Persian rug

---

[7] Yunis Bahri: A pro-Nazi newscaster who broadcast from Germany during World War Two.
[8] Famous Yemeni singers of the time.

and lit a lamp which, from its circular flames, I knew to be an *aleph* lamp[9]—we'd had one at home which my grandfather had brought back with him from the Lahaj campaign[10] to use by his divan. It would only be lit during the month of Ramadan, and was one of the things the soldiers and cavalry guards had confiscated when they came to our home.

My friend began to operate the big gramophone, which was made of ebony, playing first one record, then another, then a third. Eventually I got bored and started yawning.

As we were going back, he started talking yet again.

"You know, don't you," I said politely, "that we're going to be together for a long time. I'm afraid there won't be anything left to talk about!"

He laughed. Darkness had fallen now, on the city and on the palace, including our room, which had no lighting except a small, rusty lantern thrown down in a corner, so caked with dust and dirt and dead insects that it was no use at all.

He checked I had everything I needed, then threw himself down on his mattress. I was utterly exhausted, and yet I couldn't sleep; my eyes were drawn to that single, small window through which a glimmer of starlight shone.

After a while I heard the sound of light, wary footsteps on the stairs. They stopped at the door of the room, which wasn't properly locked—then there was a moment's silence before I heard a soft voice calling out:

"My love . . . my handsome one . . ."

---

[9] *Aleph* lamp: A kind of kerosene lamp.
[10] Lahaj campaign: A Yemeni campaign, led by the Ottomans, against the British, who were occupying the district of Lahaj in Yemen.

Holding my breath, I wrapped my blanket round my head. I sensed my companion had sat up. Then the voice came again, but this time it was inside the room. I supposed he'd risen in agitation, but he just said calmly:

"Who is it? What's the matter, Zahra?"

She didn't answer, but I sensed she'd moved closer to him, then sat down beside him.

"Can't you see I have a guest tonight?" he said.

"I know," she answered. "What possessed you to bring him here to sleep with you? There are any number of rooms in this palace, as many as there are days in the year."

He didn't answer, but I felt she'd moved even closer to him, and her whisperings changed to an excited hissing. He tried to push her away, saying that I was there, but his efforts were all in vain, and soon the hissing sound was coming from both.

I'd never felt so frightened in my life as I did that night. After a while the hissing stopped, and she gave him a kiss which—to his annoyance, because he was afraid I might be awake—resounded round the room. Then she slipped away.

I sensed him coming up to me. Then, reassured, he settled down to sleep, and soon he was snoring loud enough to drown all the roosters and all the city dogs—which made it even harder for me to sleep.

At dawn the voices of the soldiers and guards resounded in the usual song of early morning:

Oh God, we seek Your blessing.
Oh God, we seek Your blessing.
Bless us with Your favor.
We call on You, oh Sublime One!

I rose from my sleepless rest, feeling as though I'd been beaten, my whole body aching. Then I opened the small window, to see an unhealthy-looking yellow haze hanging over the city.

My friend had already got up and tidied his bed, and now he came back carrying a small coffee pot. He wished me good morning, smiling as usual.

"I hope you slept well," he said.

I nodded, rearranged my clothes and went with him to the soldiers' post at the main gates of the palace. This, I felt, was the right place for me till I began to feel less lonely.

The troops were a mixture of regular and reserve soldiers, and they carried Mauser rifles. The regulars were organized and disciplined, this being evident from their appearance, and also from their sleeping places and the way they ate and drank. Their quarters were to the right of the gate, and above them was a room where the *bourezan*, or bugler, lived; he'd settled there permanently, it was said, refusing to obey even the Governor's own orders to move out.

The quarters of the reserve soldiers were outside the gate to the left, overlooking a large square where, on the far side, a huge *toulqa* tree soared up, shading a fountain topped by a small white dove, and also a small paved area where the Governor, together with his soldiers, clerks, retinue and servants, heard the daily petitions of his subjects.

The soldiers greeted me, regulars and reserves alike, with a frank hospitality which amazed my friend. Apparently they were from my own part of the country, and they knew my family, and who I was.

I leaned against a stone set there for the purpose and watched as life began to stir in the palace courtyard and the buildings round about it, some of which were the living quarters of the Governor's relatives. It was surrounded by a high wall, with only the branches of the tallest trees visible over the top.

Windows began to open, with a grating sound sometimes, and from them peered out a strange variety of women, some with curly hair, others with their heads covered.

The soldiers had greeted my friend the *duwaydar* with their traditional song:

Your mother, oh *duwaydar*, is distracted by her loss;
Her tears fall like rain . . .

How I admired his energy and grace, and the smile which accompanied them! He was bright, quick and tactful, always ready with a witty remark, and he understood the character of everyone in the palace and its surrounding buildings: men, women, children, the regular and reserve soldiers and the *bourezan* too. He'd buzz around like a bee, from the palace to the surrounding buildings and back again, then sit down for a while with his usual smile on his face, then get up and start hovering and circling again.

Some of the soldiers sat round me, inspecting me carefully, while others gaped at me with wide, stupid grins. I didn't feel they were strangers, because there'd been people like them, colleagues of theirs, in the hostages' prison at the al-Qahira fortress. I'd enjoyed their company, because most of them were from my region, as these men seemed to be. They knew my family, my tribe, whose son I was.

I'd dreamed, longingly, of becoming a soldier like them, even if only a reserve—of carrying a rifle and cleaning it every morning as they did—of decorating it with pieces of silver or brass, or patches of embroidered cloth—of oiling it with fat from the bone marrow of rams—of using my authority over the populace, with all the profits that brought.

The *bourezan* looked out from the top of the steps leading to his room and greeted his colleagues with a call on his brass bugle. He was handsome, with the vitality of a young man, even though he was now past sixty, or even older. He was the only man without a beard, and his proud mustache was dyed with henna. His spotless clothes were of his favored white color, and everything about him was arranged in total harmony, from his turban to the traditional shoes he wore so proudly, in contrast to his barefoot colleagues from the regulars and the reserves and the artillery troops. He was the only one, in fact, who owned a pair of Adeni shoes, and they made a noise that set your teeth on edge—it reminded me of the starch being added to the milk pudding during Ramadan!

I watched him lock the door of his guardroom, then spin round to face us like a jaunty bird. The rifle slung over his left shoulder was embellished with silver ornaments and foreign coins pierced through the middle, and he had a side dagger with a genuine Sayfani blade tightly fastened round his waist. His ammunition pouch, filled with shining new bullets, hung down in front of his left shoulder and behind it, while, dangling from his waist and resting on his right thigh was his brass bugle, decorated with strips of golden cloth. Beneath the spotless cloak, which fell only to his knees, the sturdy muscles of his hairless legs were smeared with oil or fat which happened to stick to his hands during his greasy meals—his Adeni shoes and his long hair and his forehead also getting their share of this.

He laid his rifle gently and carefully on the walls by the gate, then sat down alongside us, looking inquiringly at me through eyes that were skillfully and strikingly made up with heavy black antimony. Then he began to sing, in a husky voice:

Your mother, oh *duwaydar*, is distracted by her loss;
Her tears fall like rain . . .

My friend was sitting there with my arm drawn through his.

"You didn't introduce me to Zahra," I said.

He gave me a long look, then laughed and let go of my arm.

"She's the Governor's sister," he said. "The unmarried one!"

"Unmarried?"

"Yes."

"But . . ."

"But what? She has her own ways of dealing with that, I can tell you!"

"I don't understand."

"She knows all there is to know about the human mouth!"

I didn't follow exactly what he meant. With a cunning smile he drew me towards Hafsa's house.

"Forget about Zahra. This is where the most beautiful of all God's creatures lives. Here in this house."

"You mean Sharifa Hafsa, the Governor's sister?"

"Yes. She's the youngest, and so enchanting every living man's snared into falling in love with her, to the point of distraction—and even death itself."

"Death?"

"Oh, yes. There was that poor son of Kamil, the Governor's favorite driver. He was supposed to have died in some accident or other, but I think he killed himself on her account. Some people don't believe it, but I do."

"Is she so cruel, then?"

"It's not cruelty really. It's just that there's such a huge gulf because of her position—and some other things too, perhaps, which I'll explain to you later."

I didn't try and get any more out of him, as we'd now reached the door, which he boldly opened. Awestruck as I was, I tried to resist as he took me by the hand up to the first set of stairs.

I expected to see Sharifa Hafsa at every turn of the long, winding staircases, but found instead that the house was full of women who were evidently servants and members of her retinue. My friend greeted them all, and, just as he'd done in every house we visited, introduced me in my capacity as the new *duwaydar*.

The topmost room overlooked the courtyard, and before it was a small anteroom on which my friend knocked with great deference, although he opened it before he'd received permission to enter. Then he led me into the room, which was furnished with carpets of a richness I'd never seen before. The curtains were drawn, and all round the whitewashed walls were shelves overflowing with silver and brass.

At the far end of the room, leaning with one out-stretched hand on the sill of a window, was Sharifa Hafsa, her curly hair showing from beneath an orange scarf, her fair-skinned body visible through the diaphanous white silk of her gown. Her other hand rested on her cheek, and she was looking down at the courtyard in total absorption. I gazed at her hand, which was adorned with gold bracelets and set off with henna and black dye, which showed round the tips of her fingers like red wax mingled with the purest milk.

She turned with the graceful movement of a tigress in repose, then adjusted her gown so as to cover her legs, while I stood there behind this friend of mine who kept embroiling me in embarrassing situations I could well do without. I noticed her looking at me inquiringly with those wide kohled eyes that shone so attractively. Then she turned towards my friend and started talking to him as though I wasn't there.

All I felt able to do for my part was to stand there, modestly and politely, behind my friend; I didn't even make any attempt to attract his attention, so that we could leave this awe-inspiring place. After a while she said, in her marvelously soft voice:

"Who is this?"

"A new *duwaydar*, Sharifa."

"Where was he brought from?"

"From the fortress."

"He's a hostage, then?"

"Yes."

There was a brief silence. I stayed where I was behind

my friend, with my eyes fixed to the floor, ready to leave the instant he gave the word.

Suddenly she approached us, her lovely body erect, like a many-colored candle whose melting promised every rapture of heavenly joy.

"What's your name?" she asked, putting out her hand and stroking my head.

I didn't answer, and my friend helped me out with a true *duwaydar*'s tact. She glanced at me, and I was transfixed; then, when I still failed to answer, she made no attempt to repeat the question, and we left. I felt as though an enormous burden had been lifted from my shoulders.

That night I tossed and turned, unable to sleep; I kept on rearranging the pillow under my head, but all in vain. I went to the window, such as it was, to gaze at the stars as they glowed, hearing the occasional barking of dogs in the distance. Still I couldn't sleep.

Still her image floated there in front of me, and my ears were filled with the sound of her husky, languid voice. I saw her wearing that smile that asked me who I was, whose son I was, what my name was, which part of the country I came from. In fact, I thought, it must have been a mere casual inquiry, which my adolescent imagination had magnified. Probably she hadn't taken any real notice of me in the way I'd imagined; indeed, it was clear she'd hardly been aware of my presence there in her room with my friend.

Yet I still saw her tall, slim figure before me, turning sinuously, like a smooth-skinned snake, or, perhaps, like a houri from Paradise. Zahra's hissings with my friend didn't worry me that night, nor did her resounding whispers that had almost driven me mad the night before. Somehow all my senses and feelings, my whole being, were suffused by Sharifa Hafsa.

*   *   *

Waking one morning, I found my friend had risen early as usual to wander about the palace and its surrounding buildings, and I made my way to the main gate where the regulars and the reserves and the *bourezan* gathered. The *bourezan* had already come down from his guardroom, dressed, as usual, like someone in the prime of youth.

"Where's the handsome *duwaydar?*" someone asked me.

When I didn't answer, a colleague of his said:

"He likes being with his friend, the hostage."

I didn't take the slightest notice of him. Another man came up to me.

"Where do you come from?" he asked.

"From the mountains," I answered.

"There are mountains all over Yemen," he said.

I didn't answer.

More came, till finally there were men all round me. I looked towards the square, wishing my friend would come.

"Are you a tribesman?" one man asked.

Again I didn't answer.

"The son of a *shaykh?* I bet you are!"

Still I made no reply.

"This is a fine sort of *duwaydar* for our Master the Governor to have working in his palace!" one of them remarked to a colleague.

"They ought to take the *duwadera* from the schools or the cities," said another.

"They don't need hostages from the fortress," said another.

The *bourezan* finished his part of the common breakfast, wiped his hands on his legs, and spoke:

"Why did they choose you?"

"I don't know."

"Why didn't you refuse?"

"Why should I refuse?"

"Because it meant being a *duwaydar*!"

"I thought it would be a way of getting out of the prison in the fortress and getting to the city."

He gave me a strange look and rose to his feet.

"You don't seem to understand what your new job is."

"What is it then?"

"You'll find out soon enough!"

A servant came looking for me, and I went back with him amid the laughter of the soldiers, accompanied by their invariable song. I walked on behind the servant, and, as we were climbing the first steps of the palace, he said:

"Our Master the Governor wants to see you."

Frankly, I didn't really care what he wanted from me. We climbed many floors till, finally, we reached the Governor's luxurious room at the top of the building, with its broad windows and the colored arches above them. He was reclining on his side, his stomach bloated, his eyes bulging and his lips hanging loose, as though they'd been attacked by some kind of malignant growth. He'd stretched out his short legs, and my friend was bent over them, massaging them gently with practiced and no doubt

43

expert fingers. The sounds of a splendid *nargila*[11] could be heard as the Governor puffed at its long stem and blew the smoke out into the air, and in front of him was a coffee pot in the middle of a white tray.

He asked me what my name was, and what my father's name was, and what part of the country I came from. My friend was kind enough to give the necessary answers, in a calm and polite manner, after which I simply stood there, while my friend remained engrossed in the task of massaging the Governor's feet.

I hardly heard the conversation between them, because I was so dazzled by the works of art and rich carpets and luxurious cushions that filled the room. There were, among other things, swords inlaid with gold and fine calligraphy covering most of the walls.

Suddenly the Governor addressed me directly.

"How old are you?" he asked.

"I don't know."

"Wasn't the date of your birth recorded in the Qur'an or in a notebook?"

"In my part of the country only learned men record the dates their sons were born."

"And your family?"

"We just record by the farming seasons."

I don't know whether the Governor was satisfied by my answer or annoyed by it. At any rate he got up from where he'd been lying. My friend stood up too, took me by the arm, and we descended the palace steps together.

"Why did the Governor want to see me?" I asked, as we approached the courtyard.

---

[11] *Nargila*: A kind of pipe in which the tobacco is drawn through water.

"Our Master wanted you to start work."

He looked at me, grinned, then added:

"At Sharifa Hafsa's house!"

I managed to hide my amazement.

"Why Sharifa Hafsa's house?"

"That's what the Sharifa wanted. So that's what the Governor ordered."

"But he didn't actually order me to do it."

"He told me, that's all."

"What do you mean?"

"Take it as an order, and do it."

"But . . . "

"You don't know my standing in the palace, my friend."

"But even so . . . "

"Don't be taken in by the way our room and our beds are!"

"Of course not."

"You can consider me the second man in the palace."

"The second man!"

"The first boy, if you'd rather!"

I bowed my head, and said nothing for a while.

"What are you dreaming about?" he said, shaking me by the shoulder.

"I was thinking . . . why did she choose me?"

"Lots of others would like the job."

"I want to understand why."

"Just a whim."

"What whim? She only saw me for a moment."

"Perhaps she liked you."

"You've done more to earn that than I have."

"She's bored with me now. She wants a new face."

45

"Is that the only reason?"

"Well, perhaps it's so as to divide my work among a lot of people."

"Including the soldiers and the *bourezan*?"

He pulled me roughly towards him.

"What do you mean?" he shouted angrily.

"They were asking about you. About the handsome *duwaydar*."

He let go of my shoulder and gazed down at the ground.

"What did they say?" he asked, smiling.

"Nothing. It's just that they didn't like me."

"I don't care what they say. They're just like old maids—like the ones in the palace and the other buildings."

"Really?"

"Haven't you noticed it? In the way they look and talk and behave?"

*   *   *

He drew me towards Sharifa Hafsa's house.

"Wait a moment," I said.

"Why?"

"Well, she didn't send for me. And I want to talk to you, too, about the kind of work I'll have to do."

"You'll be a *duwaydar*."

"I don't understand."

"A *duwaydar*, that's all."

"You mean . . . a servant?"

"A bit higher than that."

"I don't understand!"

"You will!"

"That's what the *bourezan* said."

"Don't worry about him. He's just an old maid too."

"Why do they call you the 'handsome *duwaydar*'?" I asked, after a brief silence.

"Because I'm handsome," he said, smiling.

"Don't play about. I really want to know."

"You'll know in time."

"That's what the *bourezan* said!"

"Well, ask him for the rest then!"

Sensing that he was getting angry, I didn't insist. After a while, he said, with a small smile on his lips:

"Don't you want me to take you to Sharifa Hafsa's house?"

"Why are you in such a hurry?"

"So that I can get the job over with."

"Is it so much trouble for you?"

"Yes, it is."

After a few moments, I said in a friendly voice:

"Will I still be in the same room with you?"

"I don't know. That's up to her."

"I want to know. It's important to me."

"She's the one who'll decide. There are better, quieter places in her house than my room. It's her decision."

"What about if you asked her? If you begged her that we could stay together?"

"Why are you so keen on that?"

"It's just what I want. Think of it as the fondness of one of God's creatures for another! Unless it disturbs your privacy."

"We'll ask the *bourezan* about all that tomorrow!"

"This business of the *bourezan* really seems to have

upset you," I said, afraid that I must have hurt him.

"Not at all."

"Then why do you keep harping on about it?"

"You're the one who started quoting him!"

*   *   *

I lay back in my friend's room, with my hands under my head, assailed by thoughts and emotions I would never have dreamed of a short time before. Then, for the first time, I saw a match being struck, lighting up the whole room, as my friend lit one of his cheap cigarettes. I sat up and crawled towards the tiny window, hoping to see something shining from the top of my lofty mountain far off; but it was pitch black, except for the glow of the distant stars. My friend broke the lonely silence.

"Do you want a puff?" he said.

I didn't follow him.

"A cigarette," he said, "to calm you down and help you sleep."

Although cigarettes had been forbidden in the fortress, where smokers were regarded as heretics and unbelievers, I'd taken a few strictly secret puffs with some of the other hostages there, in places like the wretched stone baths, where the *faqih* and the guards would never have thought of looking. Then it had made me feel dizzy, ready to faint even. But that was no obstacle tonight—a bit of dizziness and stupor was what I needed, to help me forget. I took what was left of the cigarette from my friend and drew on it till I almost burnt my fingers.

It left me floating in a daze, and all I could remember next morning was that my friend hadn't stayed there with me, because two women, neither of them Zahra, had taken him and sat on the palace steps, kissing him and squeezing further pleasures out of him. When he came back, I remember, he slammed the door violently behind him, then sank down to sleep more deeply than I'd ever seen him sleep before.

How difficult it was to wake up in this city, so different from the fortress in the mountains, with its fresh, invigorating air! In the city, you always seemed to wake with the feeling you'd been beaten black and blue, with your body swollen like a drum or the stump of a palm tree and your eyes drooping. From the very beginning there was a lingering feeling of nausea and depression, and you didn't usually feel the least desire for breakfast or coffee. All you wanted was cool water, and that was only to be found, if at all, in the soldiers' jugs.

Nevertheless, my friend got up early as usual, even though he'd been racked all night by fits of hoarse coughing. His face had become pale of late, and his body, which seemed to be getting gradually weaker, had taken on a kind of sickly yellow color which suggested some deadly disease was imminent. For my part I went cautiously off to the main gate where the soldiers usually met, sitting in a quiet corner not too close to their stupid comments and mocking song. My friend arrived before they'd noticed me there, and I saw them greet him with a cordiality which appeared somewhat overdone, and which they accompanied with their everlasting song. My friend was beside himself with rage at the *bourezan*, and in the end this became so obvious that the soldiers had to intervene. I smiled at him, but he took no notice, and drew me towards Sharifa Hafsa's house.

"Why are we in such a hurry?" I asked him.

"I want to get this job over with."

"And what happens after that?"

"We go our separate ways."

"Does that mean you're tired of my company?"

"No."

"Be frank, please."

"I am being frank. Do you think I'm not?"

"Then why all this rush?"

"So I can finish the job I've been given."

"You want to be rid of me, don't you? It's as if you were leading me off to the slaughterhouse!"

"That's not fair to me, or to her either. She's the soul of generosity."

I climbed the stairs behind him as I had the first time, but this time my feelings were quite different. I felt apprehensive and alarmed, like a rare bird about to be put in a golden cage for life.

My friend opened the door as usual, and, as usual at that time of the day, Sharifa Hafsa was looking out over the courtyard. She turned with a serious expression on her face, then stood up and came over to us, smiling at my friend and paying no attention to me. She took him by the hand, and, as I watched them, led him off into a small room. I stood there gazing into space; and, as the moments dragged heavily by, I was suddenly seized by a sense of fierce, surging pride which I hadn't felt since I was ordered to leave the fortress and come to the city.

She came back, walked past me without a glance, and returned to her favorite spot overlooking the courtyard. Then she leaned back and spoke.

"What's your name?" she said.

"You were told that yesterday," I replied.

She gave me a sharp, angry glance.

"How old are you?"

"I don't know."

"Didn't your father record your date of birth in the Qur'an, or a notebook, when you were born?"

"No."

"That's very odd."

I didn't feel like repeating to her that in my region only learned men and a few important people recorded such things in the Qur'an or tattered old books, and that my family, like all the others who tilled the land, were only concerned with the farming seasons.

This business about dates of birth seemed to be an important one in the lives of these exalted people in the palace and its surrounding buildings. It reminded me of the way the *faqih* at the fortress had talked about the *tawashiyeh* and the *duwadera*—and about knowledge and the age of puberty!

There was a brief silence. She stood up, and I lowered my eyes at the sight of her striking figure.

"Come with me," she said in an affectionate tone of voice.

I found myself following her.

"I'll show you round the house," she went on.

"I know it already," I said.

"Who showed you?"

"My friend."

"The consumptive *duwaydar*?"

"The handsome *duwaydar*."

"He doesn't know the things I want you to know . . . the things I want you to understand and follow strictly."

I was too shocked at the brutal way she'd referred to my friend's illness to reply. For the first time she looked at me closely.

"Does this friend of yours . . . know what I want from you?"

Again I didn't reply. For the first time she took me by the hand, drawing me towards the staircase, and it was as though an electric current had surged through me where she touched me. We went from the lower floors up onto the roof, and to the kitchen which was perched on the top of it, with its own storeroom for provisions.

The sweat poured from my face, as my hand remained in hers, clasped in her hand that was encircled by finely engraved gold bracelets, till it felt paralyzed there.

We went round the whole house. Her manner was full of gaiety, even when she met the old women of the family and some of her servants and retinue on the stairs, or in the various places she showed me.

* * *

The days passed; and, in spite of my work in Sharifa Hafsa's house, I felt depressed and bored and tired.

I still saw my friend—the handsome *duwaydar* as some liked to call him—and we'd spend some enjoyable moments together in the courtyard, or, according to our morning custom, with the soldiers and the *bourezan* at the main gate, where they'd sing their usual song.

We'd come together, too, in the room we still shared, each absorbed in his own daily affairs; and we'd meet in the maze of stairways and rooms, and in the courtyard of the palace and its surrounding buildings—in the kitchen, too, and in the company of the Governor's family and staff and retinue, and in the actual room of the Governor, who, right from the start of the morning, would be reclining on his left side. And in the end we'd sleep peacefully together again in our room.

One day, when I was beginning to find the life unbearable, I tried to persuade my friend to go out into the square, and from there into the city—into the market and the streets.

"I'd like to go and walk in the city today," I said urgently. "Just for an hour."

"Why?"

"Just today! Just for an hour! Won't you please come with me?"

"Is there anything you don't find in the palace and the other buildings?"

"It's not that! I just want a breath of air."

"There's plenty of air here."

"I'd like to walk with you—breathe a different sort of air—see people. I'd like to find someone selling onions or garlic or potatoes in the market who comes from my village, and ask them how my family is!"

"Your father's fled, and he's stirring things up by attacking the Imam in the newspapers in Aden. And your village is in a bad way."

This made me thoughtful. I hadn't realized my father was so important.

"As for your uncles and the other members of your family," he went on, "they're all in prison."

Again I pondered this. And I'd thought I was the only one who was a hostage in prison!

"All that's left in your houses is the women and babes

in arms—along with the Imam's soldiers and the cavalry guards."

I looked at him long and hard, and realized he wasn't making it up. Perhaps he'd picked it all up from cronies of the Governor's, or even from the Governor himself. No doubt he heard a lot of things I didn't have the faintest idea about and would never even have thought of!

"I'd like to reassure myself about them," I said quietly.

He was silent for a moment, gazing down at the ground. He seemed to regret what he'd said, or feel a sense of shame about it.

"Aren't you comfortable here?" he said.

"Yes, in a way."

"Then why do you want something more?"

"I want a breath of fresh air—to feel I'm free."

"You're a hostage of our Master the Imam."

"But I'm not a slave."

"You're a *duwaydar*!"

I looked at him, feeling a touch of anger.

"But I'm not the 'handsome *duwaydar*'," I said.

*   *   *

Our manner towards one another remained cool for several days. I felt that he was trying to talk down to me from a position of authority; but as far as I was concerned any standing he had was nothing to me, since I was in the entourage of Sharifa Hafsa and was therefore further up in the hierarchy, or so I imagined, and had more influence—provided, of course, I was prepared to go along with her wishes.

Yet something drove us to make it up quickly. One day

he took me by the hand and led me to the main gate, then out into the unpaved courtyard where the giant *toulqa* tree stood in the middle, giving shade to the throngs of disputants, petitioners and people asking favors of the Governor. Next to it stood a platform built from strong limestone slabs, and behind that was a row of rooms looking out onto a single passageway that was shaded by the roof and by the dilapidated wooden columns of a balcony which people called the "court"—that is, the place where the Governor, together with his clerks, legal experts, financial officials and the rest of the people needed for his limited work, actually met with the subjects and with citizens who had grievances. All this overlooked the city's waterway which flowed down from the mountains, bringing with it all the discarded scraps of the small world it had left behind, from yellow leaves to worn-out pieces of cloth from the clothes of mountain women and girls.

We walked towards the center of the city, amid air choked with the smell of disease and the smoke from kitchen stoves. Everywhere were faces of a pale, sickly yellow, bellies swollen not from food but from sickness, feet bare and sticky with dirt and cuts. At every corner, in every alley, square or street, we jostled amid crowds of exhausted beggars and people sick or mad.

The city had always seemed so lovely in its morning splendor, when we looked down over it from the walls of its al-Qahira fortress, the home of hostages and cannons. Sitting there, with our legs dangling from the walls, we'd see the minarets, the white domes, the houses packed within the strong outer walls, the hills and the plains and the mountains stretching as far as the eye could see.

Now, in the midst of it, in its very bowels, I saw it for

what it truly was: a pit of plagues, teeming with the sick, the mad, the deformed, the simple-minded—and with oppressive rulers; a joyless, utterly wretched city. Each day countless funerals passed through its gates, accompanied by the voices of the children and their *faqih* teachers, and of those seeking forgiveness for the dead and heavenly reward for themselves.

I found no one from my home town, since it wasn't the day of the weekly market; and so we returned. As I entered the palace gates, I heaved a sigh of relief, vowing never again to go into this city, even on market day; anywhere else, but not there!

It had been so lovely from the heights. How hateful it seemed to me now, like a living graveyard—but without the graveyard's peaceful silence.

The next day was the first day of Ramadan, and this was evident from the huge preparations and shared preoccupation of all the inmates of the palace, from the masters down to the soldiers and servants. Even my friend had filled our room with strange objects that looked as though they were made of silver; a kind of lantern, he told me. First he cleaned them, then he filled them with kerosene, then he changed the soft wicks, which were many-colored like a rainbow. Then, finally, he tried them out. How I marveled at the clear milky-white glow, and how my friend laughed at me and enjoyed my amazement at the wonderful things he was showing me!

I called back to mind the nights of Ramadan in my own home village that nestled within the folds of its proud mountain, set amid the dozens of other villages and the hundreds of terraced fields. I thought of the many thousands living there from the fruits of the land, among them those who'd been my friends and companions from the day I was born to the day I was seized and carried off to the fortress of the hostages. From the mosque we'd go to the *diwan*, the reception room of the wise men, where we'd spend the night listening to verses from the Holy Qur'an and memorizing them by the light of an oil lamp with blazing cotton wicks. If anything else was read out, then of course it was from the boring book of births, deaths and weddings!

At the fortress Ramadan had always followed the same pattern for the soldiers and their commander, and for the *faqih*, and for me and the other hostages too. We'd stand close to watch the firing of the cannons at sunset, then we'd break our fast and go quietly off to bed, waking in the morning, when the soldiers and their commander and the *faqih* were still asleep, to play amid the open spaces and passageways and high places overlooking the fortress. We took delight in picking prickly figs from the trees that overhung a precipice, reaching for the fruit with the greatest care for fear of falling into the dreadful, bottomless depths.

In the Governor's palace and its surrounding buildings, the atmosphere of Ramadan was utterly different from what I'd known before. Here every room was flooded with the milky white lights of the brilliant silver-colored lanterns. The Governor's reception room was thronged with visitors nightly, and there'd be deep discussions there on poetry and literature and politics, together with less serious exchanges that only rarely ever took an indecent turn.

As for the women of the palace and the surrounding

buildings, they had their nightly visitors too, mostly from their neighbors and from some of the aristocratic families. On some nights they'd be surprised by a visit from the women of the royal family, from the palaces of the Crown Prince, their perfume overwhelming the smell of the smoke rising from the *nargilas* and stoves.

Even the soldiers and the youthful *bourezan* had their usual place by the main gate specially prepared for this Holy Month, and there they'd discuss things together and give exaggerated accounts of battles against the Turks and the Wahhabis[12] and the British.

It was clear to me that Sharifa Hafsa must be fasting, because she'd sleep in after long nights of sitting up, waking at different hours, but always very late. This upset me, because someone like her shouldn't, I felt, be permitting herself to take risks with her health, and so risk affecting the glow of her beauty, especially during the month of Ramadan, when life's turned upside down. Still, though, her voice remained unchanged, bewitching me with the force of a powerful spell.

Throughout the Ramadan she had me delivering constant letters to a regular night visitor at the Governor's reception room. This was a man I hadn't met before, though I'd caught a glimpse of him once at one of the public or private occasions. I'd hand him the letter, then wait. Sometimes he'd write at length, so forcing me to refill the *nargilas* of some of the guests in the reception room, which wasn't really my job. Then, perhaps, he'd give me a sidelong wink, and I'd go up to him to fetch his letter back to Sharifa Hafsa. One night he pressed a silver

---

[12] The Wahhabis were followers of Saud, who practiced their own brand of Islam, and who founded the Saud dynasty that now rules Saudi Arabia.

riyal into my hand; never before had I held one, or even known what shape it was. It was as though a moon had suddenly come down to me from the sky!

When I took these written replies back to Sharifa Hafsa, she'd order me, usually, to stay with her while she read them. Some she'd tear up angrily, and only rarely would she keep one.

One night, while we were lighting the lanterns for the nightly receptions in the palace and the other buildings, I told my friend I was tired of delivering letters and presents.

"Sharifa Hafsa will get tired of it too," he said.

"Why?"

"This man's the personal poet of the Imam and the Crown Prince. He's handsome and rich, and he gets dozens of letters like that, hundreds even—from inside the palaces of the Imam and the Crown Prince and the other royal princes. They come in countless numbers. And he's so showered with precious gifts he's able to live like the Imam or the Crown Prince themselves, better even. And better than this Governor too."

"Does Hafsa—Sharifa Hafsa, I mean—know all this?"

"Oh, yes, she knows. But her own haughtiness and pride make her keen to keep up relations with him."

"Does he love her?"

"The only person he loves is himself."

"And what about her?"

"She dreams . . . but she doesn't love."

"I don't understand."

"She dreams of glory and she loves the challenge of the situation."

Sharifa Hafsa never grudged me anything, and she

59

gave me spotless clothes that made my appearance worthy of her and of myself. Yet I wanted more than this; and when I showed it, she'd become haughty in the twinkling of an eye.

One day I'd simply had enough.

"I beg you to excuse me," I said, "from the task of carrying these letters."

"Why?" she asked.

"Because it's no use."

"How dare you speak to me like that!"

"I'm only telling things as they are. He has other things on his mind."

"Be quiet, you . . ."

With her soft and lovely hand, dyed with henna and adorned with gold bracelets, she gave me a slap in the face which I took calmly, without flinching.

"You dream," I said, "but you don't love."

"Be quiet!"

I rushed down the stairs, pursued by the furious curses she was shouting after me.

* * *

A soldier took me to the main gate, and there I squatted on the ground and stretched out my leg for him to put an iron fetter round it. Another soldier banged the fetter shut. Then I walked to our room, where my friend advised me to put pieces of rag round my legs, so they wouldn't rub against the chain and cause chafing and wounds.

I said nothing to him that night, so as to preserve my dignity, but from the expression on his face he seemed upset. He confirmed that I'd been fettered on the orders of the Governor, and on the insistence of Sharifa Hafsa.

Yet in this city, and perhaps in the whole country too, the chained prisoner had a more comfortable life than the people who were free! He had no work and no worries. What work can a helpless, fettered prisoner do, after all?

I'd wake up early, which I never normally did, and go, in my chains, to the soldiers' quarters by the main gate, where I'd share their usual breakfast of stale bread and peas (if they were available), or any spiced tomato paste I could get, and chat with them about the usual things.

I wasn't talking much to my friend, but I sensed something urgent and joyful in the way he was behaving, and unusual activity in the palace and the other buildings as a whole. I asked him what it was all about.

"The Governor's son's coming back today, from abroad," he answered happily.

"But why all this noise and bustle?" I said. "Does he have a large retinue coming with him?"

"No, but he's bringing a car, his own car! It'll be carried to the edge of the city on the backs of camels, then, when it gets there, the Italian engineer will put it all straight back together again. Don't you think that's worth all the din and running around you've been seeing?"

"But surely it's an ordinary enough thing for the Governor's son to come home from abroad!"

"I'm not talking about that. I mean the car coming, his own, personal car! Don't you know what a car is?"

*   *   *

The main gate was opened as far back as it would go. Necks were craning from every window, inside the palace and outside, and the turmoil was growing. Crowds of people, colleagues or employees of the Governor in the city and countryside, had gathered, and there was a throng of men, women and children assembled in the City Square below the palace. The soldiers were organizing these in a haphazard way, and countless numbers of God's creatures were hit and punched and beaten.

I went out in my iron fetters and sat on the edge of the fountain in the middle of the palace courtyard, hoping to see my friend alongside the Governor and his returning son, and to see him riding next to them, in that small, strange car. The spot I'd chosen gave me the best possible view. I gathered up my fetters, hugging them between my knees.

I found myself, for some reason, suddenly recalling my solemn vow never to return to Sharifa Hafsa's house, however long I was kept in chains. All at once, I heard her voice behind me.

"Outside!" she was shouting. "In the courtyard!"

I neither turned nor answered.

"Gazing at God's creatures as though nothing had happened? Ha!"

Again I made no response, either by word or gesture. She shook me roughly by the shoulder.

"Why don't you answer me?"

Still I refused to respond.

She came and stood in front of me then, blocking my view of the main gate with its crowds of people who, like me, were waiting to see the coming event.

Although she was in the palace courtyard, she had her black cloak wrapped around her, and nothing was visible except her brilliant eyes, black with kohl, and her nose showing sharp as the edge of a sword through her veil. Stretching out her hand, adorned with gold and colored with the dye that set off the rosy whiteness of her fingers and the back of her hand and her arms, she seized me again, forcing me to face her.

Caught off balance by this sudden attack, I tried to stand up, but she stopped me with a quick, imperious movement of her hand and the commanding tones of her husky voice.

She contemplated me gently and at length, while I sat there submissively, oblivious now to the crowds and the coming event, overwhelmed by emotions I'd never known before.

She sat down beside me on the edge of the fountain, arranging herself in such a way that she was almost pushing me off onto the ground. I adjusted my position, respectfully, so as to give her the chance to be more comfortable. She fidgeted a little, then looked at me.

"Why did you hurt me like that?" she said. "After the kind, generous way I treated you!"

I felt as though she was addressing me like a naive little orphan.

"I didn't do anything to hurt you," I said.

"You were rude and boorish and cruel, like some ignorant tribesman."

"I may be a tribesman—but I'm not ignorant."

She slapped her leg against the side of the limestone-encrusted fountain, then placed her hand under her buttocks.

"You hurt me," she said.

"How, in heaven's name?"

"I trusted you."

"But I didn't betray your trust!"

"You forgot your position."

"I was only trying to advise you."

She turned towards me with a touch of anger.

"You're not my guardian!"

"I know. I'm just a *duwaydar*."

"Exactly! And a *duwaydar* should know how to do his job."

"Like the handsome *duwaydar*."

"You're handsome before you're a *duwaydar*."

These words, uttered in that soft, husky voice of hers that made her different from all the other women in the palace, rang in my ears. Her voice always had a sweet and magical effect on me, which left me enamored, and sounded in my ears day and night, whether I was awake or asleep.

There was a flurry of movement and voices rang out, and I knew that the procession of the Governor, with his son and the car, had come. The *bourezan*'s bugle blared out the Turkish call that announced the Governor's arrival. Sharifa Hafsa leapt to her feet, then, with a glance at me, lowered the veil over her face and sprang towards her house like a young colt, without taking the slightest notice of the approaching procession.

The crowd cheered, and for the first time I could hear the roar of the car's engine and the sound of its horn, mingling with the sound of the *bourezan*'s bugle. I stood up as the procession finally made its appearance, headed by the *bourezan*, playing loudly, after which came a group of regular and reserve soldiers, followed by some of the Governor's retinue and servants. Then the car appeared, driven by the Governor's son home from abroad; he was blown up like a frog, his eyes popping, his false smile almost lost in the swollen veins of his neck. Beside him sat his father, the Governor, dressed in his best clothes, and behind them stood my delighted friend, gaily greeting people and joking with them. I applauded him and shouted out his name—I even cheered him. How I managed to do it I don't know. The soldiers roughly threw out the city children, who were eager to see this car which had come there from some mysterious other world, then locked the gates.

The Governor's frog-like son stopped the engine, then the Governor himself climbed out. My friend leaped down after him like a gazelle, smiling as he saw me applauding him. Meanwhile the Governor's son reassured himself about the car, which was put in the stables.

There was great celebration that night for the arrival of the Governor's son. I sat up for a while with the soldiers, enjoying the sight of their popular dances to the sound of pipes and drums. They were playing their parts in the festivities, in the expectation that the Governor would reward them next morning by giving them authority over the subjects who were late paying their alms tax and other dues—which would mean profit for them. Every soldier went to bed that night dreaming of the power he might be given over the people in the particular region he wanted, knowing well enough just how much that power would yield.

*   *   *

Early next morning I was taken by a soldier to the room where the chains were to be removed. He was the only soldier left there, in fact, because the rest had all dispersed to become the unwelcome guests of the people according to the orders they'd been given. Even the *bourezan* had gone this time, with a warrant of authority to collect a whole year's dues from an oppressive *shaykh* in a fertile valley.

The soldier ordered me to sit down to have my chains taken off. I tried to question him about it, but he stayed silent, sulking at his bad luck in not going with his colleagues. Then my friend arrived, smiling as usual.

"Sharifa Hafsa's given orders for you to be unchained," he said.

"I didn't ask her to."

"Those are her orders."

"Well, I won't go along with them."

"The soldier will!"

"I'll resist."

"That could cost you dear."

"I don't care."

I'd come to a firm decision on this, and I was resolved to carry it out. The soldier tried to subdue me by force, and threw me to the ground, but I went on resisting, and in the struggle that followed I used every means I could think of—scratching him, throwing pebbles in his eyes, biting him; but he was in an even worse temper than I was, because he'd been left behind, the only one not to be given any authority over the subjects, and he took all his fury out on me, dealing me a wealth of kicks and savage blows. My friend immediately intervened on my side, but a group of men and women servants had already gathered to help break up a fight which had started, as far as they were concerned, solely because of my unjustified stubbornness.

My friend took me—still in my chains—to our room,
where he did his best to clean off the blood, bandage
some minor wounds and calm me down.

*   *   *

People were still celebrating the arrival of the Governor's
son with his matchless car. I stayed in our room, where
my friend provided me with everything I needed. I felt the
deepest affection for him, wondering at all the endless
trouble he was taking.

In spite of everything that had happened, Sharifa
Hafsa, with her figure and her voice and her countless
charms, never once left my thoughts. Day and night I
fought to drive her image from my mind; but it was
useless. I tried to recall my father and mother, my
brothers and the rest of the family, in the hope that their
images would put hers to flight, but all to no avail. She'd
become part of the room, part of my very existence day by
day. No movement was possible, or any rest either, without her presence in front of me, and even my friend's
meetings with the women of the palace and their intimacies with him no longer bothered me in the slightest.

But one night, not very long after all these things had
happened, I heard a voice calling to my friend which
didn't belong to one of his unmarried lady friends—a
soft, husky voice which made my whole body quiver.
I wrapped myself tightly in my blanket, holding my
breath.

"*Duwaydar! Duwaydar!*"

My friend jumped to his feet, terrified. He obviously
hadn't been expecting this.

"Who is it? Yes, I'm coming. Welcome!"

"I want to see your friend."

"He's asleep."

"Well, wake him up."

"Come in please."

"I told you to wake him up."

He came fearfully up to me, trying to wake me.

"Get up! Sharifa Hafsa wants to see you!"

"I'm not getting up."

"She wants to see you."

He started prodding me; and, though I did my best to make the two of them realize I didn't want to see her, I soon had to jump to my feet. She pulled me by the arm and, without a word, I accompanied her down the palace steps, making a dreadful noise as I bounded behind her in my clattering iron chains.

"I don't suppose you've ever been in chains before," she said.

I didn't answer.

"If you had," she went on, "you would have had the sense to protect your legs with pieces of rag, which would also have prevented all this wretched clattering!"

I remained silent, determined to make the chains as noisy and irritating as possible.

As we came to a halt in the courtyard, I made an attempt to ask her why I'd been fettered—to ask her why I loved her, and why she was attached to me and interested in me, and why she'd taken the risk of bringing me through the courtyard in chains. But I didn't dare, and simply followed like a dog obedient to its master—or, rather, perhaps, like a dog that was lost.

She told me to sit down next to her on the ground.

68

"Why did you refuse to have your chains removed?" she said.

"Because they meant I didn't have to do jobs I didn't want to do."

"Are you sick?" she said, clearly not understanding what I meant.

The question took me by surprise.

"Perhaps," I said cleverly.

"And lazy too?"

"I don't think so."

"Are you proud that you used to be a hostage?"

"I'm still a hostage!"

"Whose hostage?"

I made no reply. I felt a sense of pride in not submitting to the role of hostage or *duwaydar*; perhaps I could become a servant now—a servant to Sharifa Hafsa. But that didn't matter to me; what was important was that I shouldn't become a "handsome *duwaydar*." That was what was annoying me. I felt she was expecting me to say I was her hostage—her handsome *duwaydar*!

I felt, too, that she respected the stand I'd taken, because she didn't try and hurt my feelings again. She walked with me to the main gate of the palace, where the quarters of the *bourezan* and the soldiers were, and called out in a commanding voice. A number of soldiers appeared, obedient and submissive; most of the men in fact were already back from their missions. With the voice of one used to being obeyed, she gave an order, and I found myself being thrown onto the ground by a group of soldiers who gently removed my chains with the aid of two iron rods mounted on a timeworn stone.

As we went back to the courtyard, she said:

"Do you want to go back to your friend or come back to my house?"

I knew there were special advantages involved in living in her house—the prospect was a comfortable and tempting one. Yet I preferred to return to my friend's room, much as I disliked his unseemly intimacies with most of the palace women, things which I regarded as sinful.

I made the choice, finally, to preserve my self-respect and to show a front of pride and dignity. And she accepted this with the wisdom of someone who understood why young boys behave as they do.

And so Sharifa Hafsa released me from my chains and left me perfectly free to choose to remain in the room of my friend, the handsome *duwaydar*—knowing full well that in future I'd carry out any tasks she set me to do. She didn't, though, try and use me again to take her letters to the Imam's poet; she used my friend instead. And though I knew of this, I made no mention of it to her.

* * *

My friend was massaging the feet of the Governor as he lay prostrate by the window overlooking the palace courtyard and the surrounding buildings. This was apparently the custom among the governors and royal princes—although I had yet to meet one of the last. I was standing alongside my friend, and the Governor was, as usual, drawing on his *nargila* while a cup of coffee stood cold in front of him.

Suddenly the Imam's handsome poet came in. The Governor heaved himself to his feet, while my friend gave a start at this unexpected entry and let go of the

Governor's legs. The two of us withdrew to the back of the room.

If the poet's arrival was so sudden and unexpected, it was because no one could simply walk into the Governor's private room unless he was a special envoy of the Imam or the Crown Prince coming on an urgent mission, or someone high up in the intimate circle of the Governor's own family.

My friend and I were unable to grasp the full implications of the conversation that followed between the two men. It started off with a set of tedious pleasantries, beginning with greetings, then moving on to enquiries about various personal and public matters, the whole thing accompanied by shallow, hypocritical smiles. The Governor's manner was easy, although he must have realized the poet had been sent on an important errand by the Crown Prince. To my friend and myself, standing there as though we were simply part of the furniture, the talk seemed to be revolving round the Governor's son's car, and its unprecedented triumphal entry into the city. The poet was conveying the Crown Prince's displeasure at the procession and the glittering show that had accompanied it.

For all his flabby body and drooping lips, the Governor was no fool; he could hardly, otherwise, have become the Imam's governor for this important city and the adjoining countryside. He gave a smile of wonderment, apparently astonished at the words the poet had uttered.

"But," he said, after a moment's reflection which could hardly have been lost on the poet, "the car's actually a present for our Master the Crown Prince—may God preserve him!—from my son and myself. It's a long story, which begins with the time I asked my son to buy it for our Master—may God preserve him!—while he was abroad. With commendable diligence he not only bought it but arranged for its delivery to the port personally, and he also thought it best to bring it to the city himself. I waited to receive him here—and you know the rest! In fact it's his firm intention to deliver it in person to our Master—may God preserve him!—and this has only been delayed by a physical indisposition from his arduous journey. He'll deliver it tomorrow morning, driving it himself. You know, Sir, how our Master—may God preserve him!—is so preoccupied these days with the problem of these so-called Free Yemenis in Aden. That's why I didn't tell him about it straightaway. God forbid," he continued, forestalling any attempt by the poet to interrupt him, "that the car should be for me or my son! We shall preserve, as long as we have breath in our bodies, the ancient custom of riding on donkeys and mules to the palace of our Master—may God preserve him!"

He paused for a second, and the poet made a further effort to speak, but still the Governor's flow continued.

"As for the crowds of people round my palace," he went on, "it was the astonishing car they came to see, not myself or my son. And you'll have noted, Sir, that it was just the common people who were there. There were no aristocrats, or judges, or chiefs, not even a small land-owner—just rabble from the streets and alleyways of the city."

The poet managed to get in a word at last.

"Yes, I understand," he said. "Good day to you. You may be sure that I'll convey all this to our Master—may God preserve him!"

"Why must you hurry away?" the Governor said. "Stay with us for a while."

"I prefer to leave. Our Master's very concerned."

The Governor walked over to a safe in the wall, and took out some objects that dazzled us with the gleam of gold and silver. These he offered to the poet, who tried to show his gratitude by refusing to accept them; but in the end he tucked them safely away among his clothes. As he left the room he glanced at us and smiled, furtively handing my friend a letter and winking at him.

*　　*　　*

My friend and I avoided talking about the poet's visit to the Governor. Yet Sharifa Hafsa's preoccupation with this pretentious poet still upset me very much. I longed to know what was in the letter, which my friend had not yet taken, and I was tempted to deceive him, for the very first time, by opening the letter without telling him.

When he went out later on his usual errands, he left his coat hanging in its place, and I knew the letter would be there. All I needed to do was take it out, skim through it, then put it back. I wanted to know what hypocrisy he was using on her, what guileful deceit, what play on her emotions. I tried, accordingly, to steel myself to take the letter, but then drew back as a sudden wave of pride surged through me. Why should I worry about this letter, I asked myself, or about Sharifa Hafsa either?

As I was still in the grip of this painful reflection and reconsideration, my friend returned, and fell into a fit of that constant dreadful coughing of his that only stopped when he actually fainted. I'd been worried about his health for some time now, ever since those bouts had started; yet still he rolled and smoked one cigarette after another, coughing all the while till he finally passed out.

* * *

For the first time I got up early, even though I'd slept very little, and, leaving my friend to make up for his own lost sleep, went over to Sharifa Hafsa's house. Depressing though that day was, a depth of feeling drove me to see her; nothing mattered now, so long as I was working close to her. As I hurried impetuously towards the house, I told myself I was simply doing my duty—even though it was so early and I knew she'd still be asleep. I sat and waited outside the door of her room.

She opened the door so suddenly she almost stumbled over me.

"Good morning—my handsome hostage," she said.

I sprang to my feet, unable to reply.

Her hair was long and flowing, her face full, her eyes large and black. Sleep had conferred a deep repose on the body so active and vital usually, and there was just a hint of a hiss in her soft voice.

"Where's your friend?" she asked.

"He was still sleeping when I left," I said.

She tossed her head to show her displeasure.

"Do you need him for something?" I said.

She hesitated, as though not wanting to tell me.

"Go and fetch a letter he's got," she said finally, in a casual tone of voice. "Bring it straight back."

I'd hardly started walking down the steps when my friend arrived.

74

"Didn't I tell you to wake me up early?" he shouted angrily.

"No, you didn't. You're always the first person to wake up in this palace anyway."

"I don't know what happened to me last night."

"It's that wretched cough you won't try and get treated."

"Did Sharifa Hafsa ask about me?"

"Yes, she did. And about the letter too!"

He said nothing, and we went back together. Sharifa Hafsa must, I thought, have overheard some of what we'd been saying, because her anger had subsided a little now. He gave her the letter, and, seizing it with an eagerness it upset me to see, she went into her room, but left the door open, which gave me the chance to watch her reaction as she read. I saw her abruptly tear it up and throw it out of the window.

I smiled, overjoyed at this unexpected outcome; she, for her part, turned to where we were standing to assign us some unexpected chores. Seeing my smile, she shot me a questioning look, but I made no comment. I simply headed for the steps with my friend to carry out the tasks I'd been given.

*   *   *

The crisis over the car ended with it being taken over to the Crown Prince's palace, driven by the Governor's son with the handsome poet sitting alongside him.

It was a pleasant time for the Governor's son, now back from Egypt after completing his studies. Not a day passed without his being invited for lunch and the afternoon *qat* session, or for dinner, at the houses of well-known families in the city or the homes of relatives and important officials. One day Sharifa Hafsa informed us that she'd invited her nephew ("the Frog," as we called him) to have dinner at her house with some of his friends. When I asked my friend the *duwaydar* why she hadn't invited *him* for lunch and the afternoon with *his* friends, he just laughed and said nothing.

It was a hard day for us, with countless jobs to do; we even helped the servant girls polish all the brass vases and candlesticks and pitchers and spittoons. The two of us arranged the dining room together, bringing in everything that was needed. Sharifa Hafsa was proud of her house, which was furnished with the richest carpets and decorated with the best brass and silver plates. After the evening call to prayers she gave me the job, all by myself, of bringing in the dishes of almonds and walnuts and setting them out around the room, together with plates, glasses and small water coolers. Then she took me by the hand to a small room I'd never been in before, and, from a locked cupboard in the wall, took a number of bottles, some holding colored liquids, others liquids that were white and scented. These she ordered me to set out in the dining room, next to the empty glasses and the dishes of almonds and walnuts. I arranged them as tastefully as possible, with a painstaking care I didn't know I was capable of, placing everything in its natural, proper setting as though I was an old hand at it. While I was doing this, Sharifa Hafsa looked into the room, then called to me with a tenderness that made me run over to her.

I stood transfixed by the door, on which she was leaning and blocking my path. I trembled as I almost ran straight into her face, round and radiant like a new moon, and the fear sweeping through me made my heart beat quicker and my mouth grow dry. In a laughing voice, mixed with that touch of huskiness that was so dear to my heart and to my whole being, she told me to come closer, and I did so. Again she told me to come closer; again I did as she asked.

Her breath was almost burning my face now. Still she told me to approach closer, closer than I'd ever been to anyone before, even to my mother. Then she took my head between her hands and kissed me on the lips, with a kiss of the deepest, honeyed sweetness. My head began to spin, and so did the whole world around me.

"I never thought you'd arrange it all so neatly and beautifully," she said.

It had happened like a flash of lightning, and I still felt awkward and confused.

"I'm happy you're pleased with it," I managed to say.

She didn't answer, but hurried away to the kitchen, and I was brought back to reality by the arrival of my friend.

"What's the matter with you?" he said. "You look like a madman!"

"There's nothing the matter," I said.

"Well, you'd better get to work. The guests will be here soon."

I could have served a thousand guests, prepared a thousand banquets, turned the whole world upside down, then set it up again in a marvelous new order!

The first guest to arrive was the Governor's son, "the Frog," with his gurgling laughter that sounded like a *nargila*, or water being poured out of a jug. With him was a group of his friends and relations, including the poet, who entered in a flood of greetings and false smiles, accompanied by shallow, hypocritical laughter and gestures that were all theatrical and fake. I sank into a state of depression the moment he arrived, but after a while this lifted—or at least so I managed to persuade myself, as I remembered what had happened with her before their arrival.

The guests took off their traditional outer clothes and white cloaks and sat down, while my friend and I stood in the antechamber where they'd left their shoes. Some of these were upside down, and my friend turned them the right way up, not out of any concern for the shoes themselves, but because of the common superstition that shoes the wrong way up meant an unlucky day, or else offended the heavens. This practice was, I knew, found in my village and anywhere that people gather; even, indeed, at the entrance to mosques.

I kept looking at this handsome, pretentious poet, whom I'd heard reciting resounding eulogies at receptions of the Governor's. Some of these had been during Ramadan, extolling the Imam and the Crown Prince— and the Governor too.

He was an impressive-looking man, with a pleasantly brown skin, a graceful body, a deep voice and a most attractive laugh which he carefully cultivated to charm the women, and, indeed, the men too.

Suddenly I felt Sharifa Hafsa shaking me by the shoulder.

"What are you dreaming about?" she said.

I was too startled to be able to look her in the face; and I discovered, too, that my friend wasn't there alongside me to give me courage and support. He must have gone off on some errand without my noticing it.

"I'm ready," I managed to stammer out.

"Take this piece of paper to the poet over there."

Hiding my sudden shock at her command, I reluctantly took the paper from her. I felt sure, all of a sudden, that the kiss that had so overwhelmed me had been a mere bribe, so that I'd carry out the task I'd refused to go on doing before, till I'd finally been placed in chains. In other words, she'd broken the solemn agreement we'd made; led me on with the kind of trick to which only the most foolish of lovers would have succumbed, then proceeded to trample on my feelings. I found myself recalling my father's gatherings, and the tales he'd told of the love of Omar bin Abi Rabia for Sharifa Sukayna bint al-Husein![13]

Well, let her hurt me as much as she wanted. I'd show her how little I cared about the shameful way she'd behaved, that I didn't come from people whose noses could be simply rubbed in the dirt! If the pride that gripped me was a hurt pride, and the dignity a wounded dignity, still these feelings had to be asserted.

"Very good, Sharifa," I said. "I'll bring you his reply."

"Good . . . my handsome hostage."

She made to take my head between her hands and kiss me, but I shied quickly away into the room before she could do it. Then, seeing that the guests had been startled by my sudden entry, I took a grip on myself.

I stood there for a few moments, till they'd started talking and laughing again, then quietly approached the

---

[13] Sukayna bint al-Husein was the famous and beautiful daughter of al-Husein, son of Ali, the fourth Caliph, and of the Prophet's daughter Fatima. Omar bin Abi Rabia was a famous 7th-century love poet from Hijaz.

poet and steeled myself to sit down next to him. An animated conversation was going on around us about life abroad, or, more exactly, life in Egypt, on which the Governor's frog-like son was reminiscing and telling large numbers of hilarious anecdotes.

Noticing my presence next to him, the poet looked at me with his bulging eyes, then brought his hand down on my thigh, rubbing it in a way I'd never experienced before.

"Welcome!" he said in his famous false voice. "How nice to see you!"

Then, when I thrust away his hand, he picked up a glass that was in front of him and politely handed it to me.

"Have something to drink," he said, "and welcome to you! It's nice to see you!"

The fetid smell from the glass made me sneeze, and I pushed it abruptly to one side. Then I shook him by the shoulder to regain his attention, so I could discharge the task with which I'd been so unwillingly entrusted. Yet again he put his hand on my thigh.

"Welcome!" he said, turning back to me.

Again I pushed his hand away, then gave him the letter. He read a few lines—just the beginning and the end—then laughed, and, with an extraordinary sweeping movement I'd never seen before in my life, brought his hand down on my thigh for the third time.

This time I thought I'd better leave it there, because I wanted to find out just what it was he was actually after. His fingers began to wander all over my thigh in a way that went beyond the bounds of decency; evidently sure of my submission now, he was moving towards my private parts themselves, seeking something I had never given to anyone, not even to Sharifa Hafsa herself.

He was clearly determined to move on with his hand, and indulge his overwhelming desire. I managed to stop him just in time, and the other people in the room, sensing this, smiled maliciously.

The cursed swine now diverted everyone's attention by starting up a discussion about an imminent conspiracy against the Imam, in Sanaa probably, spurred on by what he called the "free people" in Aden. Cleverly, he managed to make it the kind of conversation in which everyone felt compelled to join, and each time it showed signs of dying down he found some devious way of keeping things going.

The Governor's frog-like son excelled himself in interpretations and conjectures and calculations, and the poet, I noticed, paid particular attention to the things he said. Everyone present fell silent at the point where he knew the limits of safety had been reached.

I saw Sharifa Hafsa in the doorway, concealing herself behind my friend, following my movements to make sure I handed the letter to the poet.

I made a show of not caring about her, or the letter, or the poet. At the poet's insistence (backed up by the Frog) I took the glass he was offering me, and gulped the contents down with feelings of nauseous disgust I had difficulty in concealing. Yet, at the same time, the drink made me feel prouder and surer of myself, made me feel I wanted to curse the whole world and everyone in it.

I went on drinking, knocking back a third glass the poet and the human frog had pressed on me. I've only kept a few scattered memories of how the gathering went after that. I remember, for example, the Governor's son standing up to dance, imitating Samia Jamal and Tahiya Carioka,[14] he said; taking a scarf from one of his friends, he tied it round his ample midriff and began to shake his belly. Then later, I recall, he sang a song he said was one of Farid al-Atrash's.[15]

I remember, too, that the din and the laughter and the loud conversations increased, and that my friend brought round trays of delicious grilled meat, and I voraciously ate one piece after another. My friend, I seem to recall, tried to take me by the arm, and I refused to go with him; and I remember Sharifa Hafsa's furious face as she followed the scene from the doorway.

I know the poet offered me another glass, but I forget whether I managed to take hold of it or whether I spilt it all over my clothes. His hand, though, ceased to wander indecently as the Governor arrived alongside us carrying a bottle with a long neck and a white liquid inside it. Foolishly, I tried to stand up as he arrived, out of respect, but the poet pulled me back down to recline next to him as before; then he offered me still another glass. This time I couldn't get hold of it, so he kept it and finally drank it himself. The Governor sat down, with the sweat pouring off his bald head onto his puffy cheeks and scraggy beard, then poured himself some of what appeared to be his favorite drink and added an equal measure of water, which turned the liquid to a rich milky white.

Never in my life had I felt as full as I did that night; and when I got up to satisfy a call of nature, I found I

---

[14] Samia Jamal and Tahiya Carioka: Two famous Egyptian women dancers.

[15] Farid al-Atrash: A famous Arab singer, who lived and made his career in Egypt but was of aristocratic Syrian stock.

was unsteady on my feet and the faces around me were double. I didn't feel well at all; it was as though I was flinging my body madly down the steps—or was it my body flinging me? I tried to stand still, to pull myself together, to look around me. The poet, for whatever reason, jumped up to help me down the steps, and I remember, with my right hand, giving him a slap round the face whose echo rang in my ears. He gritted his teeth, then went back to the room, while I headed for the fountain in the palace courtyard, trying, unsuccessfully, to whistle a popular tune. I threw myself onto the edge of the fountain, and all I remember after that is my friend pulling me to my feet and dragging me off to our room.

What a night it had been, and how different from anything I'd ever known before! It ended with my friend helping me to vomit up what was in my stomach.

*   *   *

Next morning I looked back on all the things that had happened. My head was heavy, and I felt I was going to vomit again. I was seized by nausea and headache together, and assailed, too, by painful misgivings and a deadly, sickening depression which refused to go away. I felt utterly ashamed. How could I ever leave this room and go and face all the people I'd been with the evening before? How could I even face my friend, who'd got up early before me as usual, and apologize to him? I felt thoroughly miserable and was overwhelmed, suddenly, by a desperate longing for my family. But after a while I put all this aside and began to confront the situation I'd been thrust into—feeling like a drowning man who clutches at his piece of straw as he fights the waves!

The day passed like a lifetime. I felt anxious, depressed and fretful, struggling against those things in my heart and my mind and my tired spirits which were now urgently driving me to embrace all the practices of my friend and companion, all the things I'd never allowed myself even to think about since I'd first set foot in this palace and its surrounding buildings. I tried my utmost, through my great pain and humiliation, to find some way out of this whirlpool; but it was all useless. What was done was done, and the outcome was inevitable now.

*   *   *

One morning my sad state of affairs was lightened by something else which had happened in the palace, and was considered a scandal so shocking that it totally eclipsed what I saw as my own scandalous behavior on that wretched, ill-starred night of Sharifa Hafsa's dinner. One man's bad luck, so it's said, is another man's good luck. The old *tabashi*[16] rifleman—may God preserve him and heal him!—had been taken off to the sole Italian doctor in the city after the Governor's female mule, a small but strong beast called Zaafarana,[17] had given him a violent kick. His bald head had been badly wounded, and he'd bled heavily and lost consciousness.

Tongues were wagging about this in the palace, and in the city as well, and the *tabashi* found himself in an embarrassing position even after his wound had healed and he'd come back to his regiment. The matter affected

[16] *Tabashi*: An artillery soldier.
[17] Zaafarana: The name means "Saffron."

all the old man's colleagues in the regiment, and everyone else living in the palace too—especially as it had come to the ears of Crown Prince Sayf.

The Governor ordered his personal stableman to sew up the pudenda of the mules and the other animals, at which my friend laughed.

"He should have given the same orders for all the women in the palace!" he said.

I thought my friend's comment was a little too outrageous, although I admit I laughed at it. And I was happy there was a topic of conversation now that overshadowed what had happened to me that night.

*   *   *

One day, after a hard day's work, my friend suggested we go and make the rounds of the stables where the mules and donkeys were kept. As we went in through the door, the old stableman was taking hay and greens round to the mules and combing their flanks with a sharp iron comb to get rid of the dead hair and kill any harmful insects concealed in the coat.

Zaafarana was swishing away countless flies with her golden-colored tail, from the top of her beautifully smooth, firm rump—flies attracted by the wounds and inflammations following the brutal sewing ordered by the Governor.

I gazed at her, wayward and alluring in spite of everything—as though she were Sharifa Hafsa!

"I don't blame him for trying," I said to my friend.

"You mean the old *tabashi*?"

"Yes."

85

"There were plenty of old maids for him in the palace!"

"He's old. None of them would have had anything to do with him."

"He could have found someone."

"I don't think so—especially with you and the youthful *bourezan* around. To say nothing of all the other young soldiers!"

"You've left yourself out. Aren't you one of us too?"

"I only love one woman—and I shall never reach her."

"You mean Sharifa Hafsa?"

"No, Sharifa Zaafarana!"

He grinned broadly, delighted by the comparison.

*   *   *

There was something like a silent feud now between Sharifa Hafsa and myself. She showed not the slightest interest in me, nor I in her, although my young heart, whose beating I could neither control nor conceal, was boiling over.

Do this, she'd tell me. Bring this. Take that. Go there. Go off. Come back. And I'd reply, as necessary: "Yes, Sharifa."

Then, on one of her scowling, angry days, she asked me, abruptly:

"Why did you slap the poet?"

The malicious question stirred me to the depths.

"It's so easy," I said, "for someone to be slapped in this palace!"

She frowned, and for a second I really imagined her with Zaafarana's golden-haired tail, swishing with it irritably and getting ready to kick me! I left hastily.

I began to join in all my friend's squalid habits and practices, plunging into his strange world so completely that he was almost jealous of me! The fact was that the women, with all their different talents and looks and figures and ages, were tired of my friend now because of his wretched, everlasting coughing, and his paleness and growing thinness, and they were apprehensive, too, about his fearful illness. And so they turned to me.

I almost pitied him—I did pity him indeed—as I watched him twisting like a wounded snake, turning his coughs into a kind of stifled hissing so as not to disturb me; and I managed to convince myself that I was protecting him by assuming some of the burdens he couldn't take on as well as he used to. Even so, I felt thoroughly ashamed of myself for the way I was behaving.

Because his bed was nearer to the door than mine, he was the one who had to open up whenever anyone came knocking, and he'd suffer agonies when he found that the person wanted me and not him. Even the Governor stopped asking for him to go and massage his feet and legs, preferring me to do it instead.

I felt really sorry at the way things had now turned round in my favor, and even sorrier when, one day, as we were down at the main gate where the soldiers and the *bourezan* and the old *tabashi* were having their breakfast as usual, he told me:

"You're to go to the Crown Prince's palace with the Sharifas today."

This had always been his job, ever since I'd arrived at the Governor's palace. I couldn't conceive what had happened to change things like this.

"What's it all about?" I asked, trying to spare his feelings. "Did Sharifa Hafsa suggest it, or is it an official order?"

"Maybe all the Sharifas suggested it. Anyway, apparently it was the Governor who ordered it."

I got up, feeling really bad about this turn of events.

"You get sent on a lot more of these trips than I do," I said, trying to pretend it was just a trivial matter, and that it was a nuisance for me to have to go, "especially to the Crown Prince's palace."

"Every man has his day," he said with a faint smile.

"That's a hurtful thing to say."

"Of course it isn't."

"You're just trying to wound my feelings."

"I didn't mean to."

"Well, that's what you're doing!"

"I'm not, really."

"You've led me astray, I know, but don't think you've dragged me down so low I'd turn on you and betray you!"

"I never led you astray. You're free to choose."

"You led me on!"

"How?"

"In all kinds of ways. Shall I remind you of a few of them?"

"I can't think of any. Don't be so suspicious about things!"

"Well, you're pretty suspicious about me."

"Of course I'm not!"

"You make hurtful remarks all the time."

"What makes you think that, for heaven's sake?"

"It's true!"

"That's enough now."

"No, it isn't."

"Everyone's looking at us."

"I don't care."

"For heaven's sake keep your voice down!"

"I won't!"

"What are you making all this fuss about?"

"To show you I love you like a brother—like a brother I've long since lost."

"Well, think of me as the brother who's come to take his place!"

"I really have thought of you as my brother, ever since I came to this palace."

"What are you getting so worked up for then?"

"Am I the one who's getting worked up?"

"Well, it's not me."

"All right, I'll get even more worked up."

"Calm down. Stop shouting like that."

"I'll shout so loud the Governor hears it!"

"I should think he has already."

"And all the people round him."

"They've picked up the echoes too."

"The whole world can hear for all I care."

"Including Sharifa Hafsa?"

"Hafsa or Zaafarana, I don't care."

"There's no need for all this."

"That way, my friend, they'll know I never betrayed you."

"That's enough now."

"No, it isn't."

"Yes, it is. Come on, let's go to our room, and I'll tell you exactly what you'll have to do."

"Do?"

"When you go to the Crown Prince's palace with the Sharifas!"

* * *

The Crown Prince's youngest wife wanted to meet the city's prominent families, and the Governor's womenfolk were naturally the first ones she invited.

They were to be taken in the one mail van the Imam had to carry the mail from the capital to the other major cities, and this had now arrived in the palace courtyard. The Crown Prince's wife was particularly interested in meeting Sharifa Hafsa because of the many rumors and stories circulating about her, which had now reached the level of wondrous legend.

I was given several heavy bundles of *qat* wrapped in the twigs of various green plants and brought from the Governor's many plantations just outside the city, which were tended by simple people who took one-third of the crop for their labor. I had to carry these bundles on my shoulder and find a suitable place for them in the rear of the van, taking great care to keep the *qat* leaves well wrapped up inside the green twigs so that they didn't wilt in the heat. Apart from drawing the curtains of the gray van when the women got in and sat down, this was my most important task. I was to stand on the back of the van, and the ill-tempered driver showed me how to put my feet on the metal plate there and hold on to the bar. Then the women arrived, their loud chatter drowning the sound of the motor and the screaming horn.

It was a really difficult job I'd been assigned, especially as I'd never been in any kind of vehicle before, let alone on the back of a van, standing there tottering between life and death! Yet I was filled with a sense of joyful exhilaration, and I found the trip an exciting one as we sped on with that frightening, groaning noise which the children had been imitating ever since this sole mail van of the Imam's had arrived in their city. And I was going, too, to see the great palace of the famous Emir Sayf al-Islam, the Crown Prince, in that village perched on its proud mountain slope which he'd chosen as his site. I was going to see so many things I'd never seen before, like the Crown Prince's guards with their blue uniforms and new German weapons, and his black slaves with their flat noses and huge, imposing bodies, and the savage lions and hyenas and tigers crouching in their barred cages inside the palace! And I'd see, too, that strange beast they called the wild Arab cow, which had, so they said, the horns of a gazelle, the head of a goat, the mouth of a camel, the hooves of a donkey, the body of a cow and the tail of a horse; its skin, it was said, combined the color of all the other animals, and it dropped a dung of strange color and shape, and fragrant smell!

I'd been told that the Crown Prince kept all these wild animals in a spot overlooking the palace courtyard, so he could amuse himself by having some of his enemies thrown into the cages. He had a particular relish for the sight, it was said—a sight which would make ordinary people shudder and turn young children's hair white, as my grandmother, God rest her soul, used to say!

It was with all this in mind that I ventured to accompany the Governor's womenfolk on that trip. I knew, of course, that Sharifa Hafsa would be among them, and that, by agreeing to go, I'd be laying myself open to snubs from her and have to follow the orders she gave me so arrogantly. Yet I felt this was an adventure I had to go through with; and in any case, my heart beat faster because of my certainty that Sharifa Hafsa would be there among the women!

The van had a special compartment in the front for the driver, and there was another alongside him. Behind this was a broad, open area covered in a rough gray material, and with a few small plastic windows on the sides which were too old and dark to let in much light. The women were to enter by the rear door of the van, which I was to close after them.

The driver was in a hurry, blaring his horn to get everyone to climb into the van. In the seat next to him sat one of the Governor's special picked men, assigned by the Governor to protect the womenfolk of the palace.

The driver ordered me, in a rude, impatient tone of voice, to open the van so that the women could climb onto the iron steps set at the back, and thence inside. His rudeness made me furious with rage, and I grew more furious still when I saw the boorish way he was standing there leering at the women's faces and very nearly devouring their bodies with his eyes.

Somehow I summoned up the courage, or the jealousy perhaps, to tick him off for the way he was behaving, for which my reward was a look of vicious hostility and contempt as he stalked back to his seat in the front. Yet I felt I had to do it, for all his hateful arrogance, and even if he did consider me a mere *duwaydar*, a hostage in the palace of one of the Imam's governors!

I raised the curtain at the back of the van with my left hand, leaving my right hand free in case I needed to help any of the women climb in, especially if they were too old to manage it on their own—there were plenty like that in the Governor's palace! They started getting in. I knew them all, even the neighboring women!

All my nerves were stretched and alert, and my naive young heart was pounding, as I waited for Sharifa Hafsa to come and climb past me into the van. Should I look at her? And if she happened to look at me and smile, should I be especially cordial and cheerful? Should I offer to do some personal service for her if she gave me the chance— help her climb into the van, or look after her cloak so that it didn't get dirty, or make sure she had plenty of room inside the van, or even spread some of my own clothes on her iron seat, or pick up her shoe if it fell off and put it back on her plump foot?

They got in one after another, and everything was going perfectly smoothly. Then, when Sharifa Hafsa tried to climb in, her right foot slipped off onto the ground so that she lost her balance, and, automatically, but with fear in my heart, I gathered her in my arms and helped her up into the van. As my hands plunged, somehow, into the folds of her body, it was as if I was touching some delightful thing, amazing and awe-inspiring, which made me tremble from head to foot. For her part, she seemed to be totally preoccupied with arranging her cloak and her make-up. I managed to smile somehow, and she responded with an awesome frown, like the frown of a young tigress.

My heart was quiet now, and so was my conscience. Sharifa Hafsa, I believed, had done what she'd just done simply to embarrass me and have me take her in my arms. That seemed logical enough, although she certainly wouldn't have wanted me to see through her ploy. But what else was I to think when she was the only vigorous young woman among all the palace women gathered there? The older women had all got in without anything untoward happening; she was the only one who'd stumbled as she climbed up!

My face reflecting the elation I felt from this incident, I drew the curtain at the back of the van, climbed up and shouted to the driver to start—although, in fact, he'd anticipated me by moving off a few seconds earlier, which might easily have made me fall flat on my back on the ground.

The van drove towards the city, with its narrow streets that had never thought anything with four wheels carrying more than one or two people would ever pass through them. It sped through the great city gate, then climbed a road paved with black stones which had been built for caravans several hundred years before, in the times of Queen Arwa. I held on to the iron bar, as the driver had told me, but not without a sense of strain.

When Sharifa Hafsa nervously opened the thick curtain, I would have fallen off if I hadn't been holding on so tightly. I looked at her firmly and tried to draw the curtain back in place.

"Leave it open!" she shouted. "We need some air in here!"

I became confused at the sound of her voice, which always had such a powerful effect on me. I tried to push the curtain up onto the roof of the van, but lost my balance, and I was just on the point of falling off when she shouted to the driver to stop. Then she tapped on his window and repeated her order.

"Stop the car!"

The bad-tempered driver obeyed, and asked the reason.

"Are you trying to kill the *duwaydar*?" she said sharply.

"Of course I'm not!" he said.

"Then let him come in and sit with us."

The picked man alongside gave his hesitant assent.

"Tell him to get in, Sharifa," the driver said.

Sharifa Hafsa took hold of the front of my shirt and pulled me down next to her. I found the whole thing thoroughly embarrassing.

The van shook on the rugged road, so that her body rubbed against mine and her breath stung my cheek. Some of the women were sick in the car, while others got involved in a conversation I couldn't understand, and which she didn't join. She kept looking at me and smiling, almost laughing sometimes; and a little later she actually did burst out laughing so loudly that the other women stopped vomiting and talking, and looked at her in astonishment—and it seemed to me that they were looking at me too. But she paid no attention to them, and they went back to their completely artificial-sounding conversation.

The sweat was pouring down my face, onto my clothes.

"What's the matter with you?" she said, nudging me with her shoulder. "You look so foolish."

I just wetted my lips with the tip of my tongue.

"You're as silent as a statue!" she said.

"This is the first time I've ridden in a van."

"Do you feel sick?"

"I don't know."

She pushed the edge of her cloak towards me and laughed.

"Do you want to be sick like some of them?" she said.

"If I need to," I said, "I'll do it outside the van."

She lost her temper suddenly.

"What's the matter with you? Anyone would think you were sitting on hot coals!"

"It's worse than that!"

"But you know everyone in the van, don't you?"

"Yes, I certainly know most of them."

"And yet you pretend to be shy!"

"I'm not pretending anything."

"You mean you've always been like that, since the day you were born?"

"Yes."

"Now don't say what isn't true. Tell me, which one haven't you slept with?"

I didn't answer.

"Is it the Governor's cousin, or the one who's looking at you as if she could eat you? She's from our family, but she lives in the country."

I wished I could just jump out of the van onto the road.

"Please," I said, "don't embarrass me any more!"

"Am I wrong then?"

"I'll get out of the van!"

"That wouldn't work. I'd follow you anyway."

"I can't bear any more of these wild fabrications."

"How dare you talk to me like that!"

"It's the truth."

"And you dare to say a thing like that to me, Sharifa Hafsa, the Governor's sister?"

"You treat me like a little child!"

"I want to see you become a man."

"I am a man."

"You haven't proved that yet!"

"Do you want me to be depraved?"

"Of course not!"

*   *   *

I thanked God for our safe arrival at the Crown Prince's palace, where I sprang quickly out of the car to make way for the women to get down. I expected Sharifa Hafsa to come out straightaway, since she'd been sitting next to me by the door, but she waited till the end.

"Don't disappear," she said as she came down. "We'll be needing you. Bring in the *qat* after lunch."

She gave her orders in a commanding voice which intimidated the bad-tempered driver and even the picked man. The other women tried to speak in the same way, but merely met the open sarcasm of the driver.

I stayed in the palace courtyard with the *qat*, not knowing what to do with myself. I could see the Crown Prince's private guards, striding about in their traditional blue uniforms and constantly shouting to one another. The Governor's picked man, who was an old man, had gone to squat by a wall, leaning against a large stone and silently chewing *qat*, though he hadn't even had his lunch yet. It was clear the Governor had chosen him well for the kind of jobs he had to do. He gave no sign of knowing me, even though we'd met at the palace, making no effort whatever to talk to me about anything. I left him in the spot he'd chosen, and went out into the spacious courtyard, trying to find the animals I so much wanted to see. I was worried, though, about the *qat*, which I'd left next to the guard. He was so fond of it he went without food to get it, and I was sure he'd secretly steal some while I was away.

I reached the enclosure reserved by Crown Prince Sayf al-Islam for the cages of the wild beasts: the lions and tigers and hyenas, animals that represented ferocity and terror. Looking then for the wild cow, I was told by one of the Prince's private guards, to my astonishment, that I'd find it outside the palace gate, browsing among the people who'd come with their problems, some of them from very remote places, and were waiting for the Crown Prince's answer.

I finally got bored with wandering around outside the palace, and began to feel very lonely. Then a huge slave, as black as night and wearing the uniform of the private guards, came towards me, accompanied by a handsome young man. I realized they were looking for me.

The handsome lad was evidently the Crown Prince's special *duwaydar*. He was a plump young man, very good-looking and spotlessly dressed.

"Are you the *duwaydar* from the Governor's household?" he asked.

Never had I felt the word *duwaydar* to be more of a slap in the face than I did that day!

I nodded, feeling bitter and resentful.

"You look as if you're a hostage from the fortress," he said, eyeing me closely.

I nodded again, and he gave a look of distaste.

"They shouldn't make hostages *duwadera*," he said.

"You're quite right," I said, in a heartfelt voice.

"Because," he went on, interrupting me before I could say more, "they're uncouth, ill-mannered boors who always run away."

I smiled as the force of his last words struck me.

"What do you want from me?" I said.

"Want from you?" he said, making no attempt to hide his malice. "I don't want anything from you at all. Sharifa Hafsa insisted I should come and fetch you. What she wants from you I've no idea."

"If it's the *qat* she wants," I said, "I left it with the old man sent by the Governor."

"We've already taken the *qat*," he said. "It's you she wants to see."

I walked after him, while the black slave walked behind the two of us. I noticed the way his plump, soft body moved through his transparent silk robe. It was as though his movements weren't consciously contrived any more, but had become a part of his very nature. We went through an open courtyard where clear waters whispered into a rounded fountain far more spacious than the Governor's. Inside the fountain was a small boat in which a handsome young lad of about thirteen years old was floating.

He steered his boat up to us and stretched out a hand to greet us, and I waited for the Crown Prince's *duwaydar*, or his slave, to help the lad climb up onto the edge of the fountain; but they took no notice of him. Feeling I ought to help him climb out of the pool, I stretched out my own hand. He took it, then suddenly gripped it firmly and pulled me violently into the pool, in which, to my great embarrassment, I landed fully dressed. I almost choked to death as the water rushed into my throat and nose, and my wet clothes were a further hindrance as I strove to scramble out of the pool and save myself from drowning.

I finally got out safely, but a wave of fury went through

me at what had happened and at the way the pampered boy was laughing his head off. Meanwhile the Crown Prince's effeminate-looking *duwaydar*, together with his black slave, was treating the lad with the utmost deference.

My only thought was to tip up the boat and its contents, and this I did with a violent heave, leaving the child struggling in the water, while the *duwaydar* screamed for help. Some of the Crown Prince's guards and slaves rushed up to us, then, to my amazement, plunged into the water, clothes, weapons and all, to rescue the boy, who was now making terrified groaning noises that seemed to be coming up from his very guts.

I was busy wringing the water from my clothes when I felt a sudden treacherous blow on my left ear and cheek, so painful that it made my whole head ring. I saw, as I looked round, that it had come from the pampered boy; and, catching hold of him by the front of his shirt, I threw him down onto the ground and started raining blows and kicks on him. I would have trampled him half to death if the guards and slaves hadn't intervened.

This day, which I'd expected to enjoy so much as I got to see all kinds of new things, or at least had a change from the Governor's palace and the people in it, had now turned into a nightmare of unforeseen troubles. I'd thought I might fall off the back of the mail van, or get crushed under the bundles of *qat*, or have all sorts of typical problems with Sharifa Hafsa, or cross paths with the handsome poet, who'd be sure to treat me in a brutal, humiliating way; I'd even thought the Crown Prince's wild beasts might come and devour me as I was watching them. But who would have expected a pampered brat to treat me like this?

I was ready for any sort of attack now, from whatever quarter—especially after some of the guards and slaves had forced me into a cell by the main gate of the palace, as a prisoner, and I'd learned that the boy was the son of the Crown Prince Sayf al-Islam, and the apple of his eye!

"What do you think you're doing, you madman?" the head guard said to me.

"What did I do?"

"You attacked the boy of our Master the Crown Prince, that's what!"

"Well, he was the one who started it!"

He was silent for a while.

"We're keeping you here as a prisoner," he said finally.

I said nothing, and he added quietly:

"Until Sharifa Hafsa gets things sorted out."

"What does it have to do with Sharifa Hafsa?" I said furiously.

"You're her personal boy, and she's responsible for you."

First a hostage, then a *duwaydar*, and now a boy!

"I'm not her 'boy,'" I retorted, "and she's not responsible for me."

"That's an odd sort of thing to say."

"What's odd about it?"

"She's gone to such lengths to help you. She even managed to see our Master the Crown Prince!"

"Did she meet the poet?"

"Who do you mean? I don't follow you."

"The handsome poet."

"Oh, you mean the *ustadh*?"[18]

---

[18] *Ustadh*: A teacher, a university professor, a learned man. It may also mean "Sir" when used in the vocative.

"The poet, yes."

"Yes, that's the *ustadh*. He sometimes teaches the children of our Master the Crown Prince."

"That may be him."

"If he's the one you mean, he's been with Sharifa Hafsa trying to defend you."

This upset me, but, fearing the head guard might sense what I was feeling, I took a grip on myself and tried to change the subject.

"What's so special about that boy," I said, "that I have to be punished because of him?"

"Hadn't you seen him before?"

"How could I have done? I'd never even heard of him!"

"Our Master, Sayf al-Islam, loves him above all God's other creatures," he said, smiling. "He favors him over his children, over all his wives, over everything in the world."

He enlarged on the subject, speaking to me in a good-natured and very kind way. The boy was, I learned, the son of one of the Crown Prince's drivers, and had some Turkish blood, his mother being Turkish by origin. The Crown Prince had become abnormally attached to him, and I gathered that there were rumors of the boy being the Crown Prince's illegitimate son—clearly a most disturbing thing for all concerned.

From his early childhood, it seemed, the boy had been allowed to play with the Crown Prince in his private room, where neither his own avowed children nor his beautiful wives were ever permitted. The Crown Prince would bow to the child's most impossible demands, and even allow him to play with his beard and mustaches, or turn his formal council into pandemonium with his screaming and shouting.

102

Afterwards, when I'd calmed down, I learned that the Crown Prince hadn't taken the incident in the terrifying way I'd feared, since Sharifa Hafsa and the handsome poet had managed to convince him that it was an ordinary incident and conceal the uproar which had seized the whole palace.

It was nearly sunset now, and I heard the head guard calling to me to get out of his prison and go back to the Governor's house in the van, along with the women.

The main topic of conversation in the van was what had happened and what I'd done, and some of the women shouted at me in those hideous voices of theirs, grimacing at me with their ugly mouths, some of them showing yellow, rotting teeth and others without any teeth at all. The way they treated me, you'd have thought I'd violated the heavens by committing some crime unknown since the birth of humanity!

I sat huddled up alongside Sharifa Hafsa, who, as before, hadn't let me stand on the back of the van, but had made me come in and sit next to her. She looked at the women without a word as they spat out their condemnation of me, full of curses and ugly epithets. She just smiled, and laughed a little from time to time, with that laugh that so fascinated and captivated me.

"God preserve us!" one of the women said. "If our Master the Crown Prince had known the truth, he would have turned the whole world upside down on our heads!"

"Let's just hope and pray our Master the Governor never hears about it," said another. "If he does, he'll be the one to turn the world upside down on our heads!"

"He'd be furious about it," said a third.

Further women added their contributions:

"God preserve us, what a disaster it would have been! But God's been merciful to us so far!"

"I don't know why we need to have this hostage *duwaydar* along with us! Just look at the way he behaves! He's no manners at all!"

I could hardly contain myself at all these hateful comments, and tried to get free of them by putting my head out of the window of the van, and then a good part of my body after it, but Sharifa Hafsa kept pulling me back next to her, smiling at the things the women were saying, and giving the occasional sarcastic laugh.

"Whatever we do, we mustn't let this get out," said one of the women.

"It was one of us who was responsible for it all," added another.

Sharifa Hafsa smiled and broke her sarcastic silence.

"For heaven's sake! Are you all blathering like this out of pity for the Crown Prince's boy or just gloating over what happened to the hostage here?"

Her resounding voice, accompanied as it was by a peal of sarcastic laughter, had the effect of silencing them. Then, suddenly, she got hold of me and threw me towards them, so that I lost my balance and fell in some of their laps.

"You're simply jealous of me," she said, "because he's sitting next to me. Am I jealous of you because he's in your beds every night?"

"Don't take yourself for Zulaykha, the Pharaoh's wife," said one of the women, managing to control her nervousness.

"Well, he's not Joseph either, you stupid woman!" Sharifa Hafsa immediately retorted.

104

I was overcome with shame at this squalid, totally unforeseen situation. In the midst of the confusion I noticed the girl from the country, who hadn't said a word, sitting crouched in the corner of the van, stunned and overcome with embarrassment.

In a flash I rushed to the back of the van, just as it had gone through the main gate of the city, and jumped out quickly into the empty street, where the shops, according to the usual decree, were closed for the two evening prayers. The only people there were some policemen, with their crescent-shaped brass insignia that dangled from their necks and their piercing whistles inherited from the time of the Turkish occupation.

I slipped into an alley I didn't know and raced headlong down it. Then, suddenly, I heard quick panting behind me, and hurrying footsteps like my own. It was Sharifa Hafsa!

She gripped my arm like a vise.

"Where on earth do you think you're going?" she said.

"Let me go, please."

"I won't let you go!"

"I'll make you. Leave me alone!"

"I don't care, you coward."

I thrust her violently aside, so that she almost fell, but she quickly regained her balance, then took an immensely strong grip on me, using both hands. Her black cloak had fallen down, giving a clear view of her captivating feminine form. I almost slapped her lovely face where the veil had dropped from it, but thought better of it.

"Well, come on," she was saying defiantly. "Hit me!"

I was stunned.

"Why don't you hit me?"

Still I could make no reply.

"Show me you're a man."

I struck my own thigh instead.

"Please fasten your cloak," I said, defeated now.

"Didn't I tell you you were still a child?" she said, laughing.

Surely she must know I was a man in reality! But I managed to control my fury. We were back in the street now, and people might well gather round us when they came out of the mosques. In fact some people had come out already.

"Please," I said, quietly and calmly, "let me go back on my own."

"No, I'm not leaving you. You're a hostage—my hostage for the moment."

"A hostage, a *duwaydar*, a boy! Well, so be it, but you're not my guard."

"I'm even more than that!"

I broke free and raced away.

"Are you going to leave me here on my own," she shouted, "when I don't know the way to the house?"

"You know the way perfectly well."

"Even if I do, what will the Governor say, and all the others?"

"They'll say you're just on another of your late-night excursions outside the palace. Some of them are much later than this!"

A stone hit me violently in the back, and I heard her husky, lazy voice raised.

"I won't let you go."

I just felt for the place where my back had started to hurt. She shouted even louder.

"I'll call all these people coming out of the mosques and tell them to arrest you."

"That would bring you a scandal."

"You're the one who'd have the scandal—because you're running away."

I said nothing, wandering on through the strange streets. She threw a second stone, which hurt me again. Overwhelmed by pain and anger, I picked up the stone and hurled it back towards her—not actually aiming at her, but to one side, as a warning to her not to take any further liberties with me. But still she didn't stop; instead she picked up a third stone and ran straight at me. I came to a halt, defiant and resigned at the same time.

She came rushing up to me with the stone in her hand—so close that I was expecting her to dash it in my face and leave me torn and bleeding. But then she hurled the stone away from her and threw herself onto me, embracing me in a way I'd never known even from my own, loving, tender mother! Then, as she bent down to pick the stone up again, she began to weep from the very depths of her heart, in a way I'd never heard her weep before—very different from those throbs of her heart which had so often moved my own loving heart and all my tenderest feelings!

Then she threw the stone violently down again and gripped me by the front of my shirt.

"What's the matter?" I said, as she went on weeping.

She didn't answer, and there was all the fragrance of paradise as she lay there against me. I tried to ease her away.

"What's the matter?" I asked again.

"Nothing."

She was silent for a moment in my embrace, then she moved away a little.

"Is it back to chains and imprisonment for me?" I said.

"They're all you're worth!" she answered.

*   *   *

With slow, plodding steps, like a prisoner of war, I followed Sharifa Hafsa through the palace gates; and the moment we'd gone in, she ordered a group of soldiers to arrest me. They put chains round my legs, and Sharifa Hafsa went on to her house.

The soldiers and the *bourezan* greeted me with broad smiles and general merriment, this being, however, spoiled by a quarrel over where I was to sleep, which the *bourezan* finally won. He took me off to his special cell, helping me as I climbed the stairs with the fetters on my ankles.

"Those soldiers are rogues," he said. "You could never be sure you were safe with them."

I nodded gratefully, not really clear why he was giving me all this personal treatment. I'd wanted to be imprisoned in my friend's room, but I hadn't seen him, and quite possibly he didn't even know what had happened to me. I missed him in this new predicament I was in, although I felt that being with the *bourezan* might well be less of a problem than staying with the other soldiers.

As soon as we'd entered the room, he laid down his rifle, spread a mattress out for me and gave me the necessary pillow and blanket and sheet. Then he took his leave, saying that he was on guard duty that night and advising me to lock the door on the inside.

I knew that, for all his many faults and his affectation of youth, he was a gallant, noble-hearted man. Even so, I suspected that he really had an assignation with one of the women in the palace. This was never actually confirmed, but when everyone was asleep that night I heard voices and cautious, furtive movements which I was sure came from him and one of the women, whose voice I couldn't recognize.

I closed my eyes and tried to sleep, after this day of most unexpected upheavals and problems. Yet sleep wouldn't come, as I tried, endlessly, to work out why Sharifa Hafsa had behaved as she had. What explanation was there for all the things that had happened, how could I convince my heart and mind they were real? Were the events of that day a matter of love, or a mere game?

*   *   *

For all my sleeplessness, I got up early next morning, as the first rays of dawn penetrated into the room. I now had a clear view of the place I'd had to spend the night in, which, the evening before, I'd entered by the faint light of a small lamp. It was a round-shaped room, and everything in it was clean and tidy and well set-out, to an extent I hadn't been accustomed to even in the Governor's own palace.

His bed was made, with the blanket neatly laid out on top of it, and his colored wooden chests were all clean despite their age. Some of his personal belongings were hung most carefully on the walls, with a marvelously tasteful harmony of color and arrangement. At the lower end of the room was a water jug, a fireplace and some brass and earthenware cooking utensils, all covered with embroidered cloths, and even his shoes had their regular place. As for his brass bugle, with all the colorful decorations hanging from it, it was hung up in a special spot and covered with a transparent silk scarf. I envied him this neat, orderly state of things, which must certainly have helped towards his healthy old age.

When I got up and opened the door, I found him asleep in a spot overlooking the palace courtyard, snoring away, with his rifle under his leg. After a good deal of hesitation, I decided to wake him up so he could finish his sleep in the room. He came to with a start, and collected his things as if he'd expected me to act as I'd done. Then he went into the room, locked the door and sank into a deep sleep.

As I swayed, in my iron chains, to the bottom of the steps that led to his room, I encountered those of the soldiers who were already awake. They made mocking faces, then broke into their usual song:

Your mother, oh *duwaydar*, is distracted by her loss;
Her tears fall like rain . . .

Taking no notice of them, I lay down by the main gate where the air was cool and pleasant, with my head on the stone set there for the purpose, and gazed out into the spacious courtyard. Soon my *duwaydar* friend came hurrying over and sat down next to me, carrying an earthenware dish on which cakes and other things had been arranged on a large number of small plates. Being familiar with the plates Sharifa Hafsa used at her important parties, I realized the food had come from her house.

110

My friend saw I was depressed, and spoke to me gently and affectionately.

"What have you been up to now, you madman?" he said jokingly.

"Nothing," I said.

"Oh, really?"

"What do you mean?"

"I've been hearing about some of the things you did yesterday!"

"She just jumped out of the van after me, that's all."

"What do you mean, 'she'?"

"Sharifa Hafsa."

"I'm not talking about that."

"What are you talking about then?"

"What else did you do?"

"I can't remember."

"They say you hit the Crown Prince's son!"

"You mean that spoilt boy who pulled me into the pool with all my clothes on, for no reason at all? I thought I was doing him a favor and saving him from drowning!"

"Yes, that's the thing I'm talking about."

"Well, it's all over now, and he got what was coming to him."

"Are you really quite crazy, or just stupid?"

"As far as that's concerned, I'd rather be crazy!"

"You must be!"

"Perhaps I'm still crazy now!"

He was silent for a moment.

"That boy's the illegitimate son of the Crown Prince," he went on, "and the Crown Prince thinks the whole world of him. He loves him more than anything else, including all his lawful children."

111

"What do you mean?"

"Haven't you grasped just how important this illegitimate son is to the Crown Prince?"

"No, I haven't!"

*   *   *

Sharifa Hafsa had ordered my fetters to be removed, and, to emphasize my importance to her, the order had been confirmed by the Governor himself! As my friend led me by the hand to the room where one of the guards was to unchain me, he began to tell me of some strange things.

"It's been quite a night!" he said.

I was busy wondering why I wasn't putting up any resistance this time as they unbound me from my chains, and didn't answer. He nudged me with his elbow.

"What's the matter?" I said.

"There were a lot of tongues wagging in the palace last night!"

"Why? Has something happened?"

"No. The talk was all about you and Sharifa Hafsa and the way you hit that boy of the Crown Prince's—and the suspicious way you were away with the Sharifa at night."

I was silent, going over the previous day's events in my mind.

"The Governor's bound to call you to see him today," he went on, "to find out exactly what happened, especially after the way Sharifa Hafsa went and defended you, and melted his heart by bursting into floods of tears in front of him. You know how much he thinks of her."

As I imagined her tearfully entreating the Governor, I was filled with awe, because she never usually wept, and I couldn't hold back the tears that sprang from my own eyes and flowed down my cheeks. If she'd really wept, speaking through her tears in that low, husky voice of hers which had always so bewitched me, then it was a wonder indeed! Brushing away my tears, I reflected how precious and important I must be to her, and what a place I'd come to occupy in her heart.

* * *

The Governor did indeed summon me, to his favorite, sumptuously furnished upper room where he sat by himself for a while every morning, smoking and peering out onto the palace courtyard, watching every movement of the subjects in this, his private kingdom.

He was sprawled out as usual, with his huge belly bulging out and his legs crossed; and, as usual, he simply didn't reply to the greeting I gave him as I entered. He looked vaguer than I'd ever seen him even at this early hour, when he was generally milder and better-tempered than at other times. I kept waiting for him to turn his eyes towards me, but he took no notice of me at all. At last I cleared my throat as one does in these situations, and he looked up.

"Hey," he said. "Come here."

I went up to where he was sitting.

"What did you do at the Crown Prince's palace?" he said.

"Nothing," I answered.

"Nothing? What about all the uproar you caused?"

"There was no truth behind it all."

"I don't believe you. You must have done something wrong!"

"Well, what was it then?"

"Are you asking me?"

"Who else should I be asking?"

"Don't be insolent!"

"I'm not being insolent."

He hurled the stem of his *nargila* to one side. Then he calmed down.

"Where did you go with Sharifa Hafsa after that?" he asked.

"We came back here."

"That's a lie!"

"Were you told something different?"

He was silent for a moment, then put the stem of the *nargila* back in his mouth and drew a little tobacco through the water.

"You stayed behind the others. The other women, I mean."

"I preferred to walk when we got to the city, because the van was so full."

"What about Sharifa Hafsa?"

"She got out of the van for the same reason, and walked back with me."

"Why?"

"For the same reason. She preferred to walk because the streets were empty for the moment."

"Even Sharifa Hafsa didn't tell me that!"

He didn't continue the argument, though I was ready for him. Instead he said, in a sharp, angry voice:

"You're never to do this again!"

I lowered my head and remained silent.

"Don't forget that! I'll be watching you in future!"

Again I made no reply.

"Now, what did you do to that boy of the Crown Prince?"

"He started it, and things just went on from there."

"Don't do it again."

"No, sir."

"Don't think you're in your own part of the country, where you can do as you like. You're here as a hostage and a *duwaydar*. Think yourself lucky I let you leave the hostage fortress to come and have a good life at my palace."

"I'd like to go back to the hostage fortress," I said.

"That's out of the question," he said in a very angry voice.

"It isn't. I've come of age."

"Don't tell lies!"

"It's the truth!"

"You don't know anything. You're just ignorant!"

"It's clear from the signs on my body."

"Not to me."

"Shall I show you?"

"You're insolent! And you're dreaming too."

"It's true. Why should I be dreaming?"

"Because you want people to say you're a man."

His words hurt me, because they reminded me of what Sharifa Hafsa had said; it was as if she and her brother were combining against me on this point.

"I'm a man," I said resentfully, "and I was a man before I ever went to the fortress or came to this palace."

The Governor lumbered heavily to his feet. I sensed that he was dismissing me, and I left accordingly.

*   *   *

Next day the Governor summoned me again.

"You're to stay here with me now," he said. "Don't go anywhere else."

I resigned myself to following his orders, but asked him, nevertheless, what my duties would be.

"You're to look after the reception room and attend to everything that's necessary there. You're a man now, after all!"

*   *   *

My friend the handsome *duwaydar* had become even paler, and his body was still thinner. Several times in the night I'd been disturbed by his hacking cough. He'd keep coughing till he almost passed out, and would only come out of his fit after I'd put my arms round him and pressed my hands on his chest, which was so weak now.

*   *   *

I stopped going to Sharifa Hafsa's house, feeling that this would be against the definite orders of the Governor, now that—as he reminded me a number of times!—I'd become a man. Even inside the palace itself I no longer went into the parts reserved for the women, even into the kitchens, or performed any services for them.

My work was confined to the Governor's reception room. I'd prepare the cold water and the censers, change the water in the *nargilas* and make the fires, and, during the daily gatherings, I'd put the burning embers on the tobacco and carry out all kinds of other tasks within this confined little world.

116

Sensing that I felt humiliated in the job I was doing now—which was a servant's work, after all, rather than work for a hostage or *duwaydar*—the Governor frequently offered me *qat*, and also set aside a place for me to sit in the lower part of the great room. Chewing *qat* now became a habit with me.

I enjoyed sitting there, listening to the discussions of current events; these would be conducted in low tones, but I'd hear phrases, here and there, which gave indications of things that were going to happen. Many of the conversations were about the Liberals and the Constitution and the Crown Prince, Sayf al-Islam, and his father, the old Imam.

The Governor said less than the others, because of his important position, perhaps, or because the conversations were taking place in his palace. But when everyone had gone home, he'd sit plunged in deep thought, as I went round clearing up the remnants of leaves and *qat* twigs the guests had left behind them, emptying the spittoons and earthenware water cups, folding up the stems of the *nargilas* and clearing away the ash. There he'd sit with his water pipe in his hand, and a big radio with a huge battery in front of him, which he'd move from station to station in the hope of catching some important news. Sometimes he'd call in my sick friend, the handsome *duwaydar*, and tell him to get down and massage his legs and feet as usual.

I longed to help my friend in this task, in view of his condition; yet it was a job I loathed and despised too, a humiliating job which I couldn't possibly imagine myself doing now. I'd take him back to his room, exhausted as he was, and help him arrange his bed. One evening I started

117

massaging his feet, but he shouted at me to stop, his eyes blazing with anger, and I did as he said.

One evening, when I came back from my usual, routine work, I found my friend asleep, or pretending to be asleep, with his blanket over his head, and saw that all the pictures on the walls had been torn down and thrown on the floor or outside the door. And there was a further surprise in store too: the few things of my own, like my bed and my blanket and my small colored wooden chest, had all been put by the door, as if he wanted me out of what he regarded as his own private room, and out of his whole world.

The light from the dirty, broken-down old lantern was as faint as it always was. Dejected, I fell to thinking about my friend, this sick young man who'd once been an active *duwaydar*, and wondering just what had happened to him and what had come to disturb our close friendship.

He could have asked me, quite openly, to leave his room and look for another one; there were, after all, any number of rooms available in the palace, many of them bigger and pleasanter than his. Once, in Sharifa Hafsa's house, I'd been offered a private, fully furnished room with four windows and with a bath nearby, but I'd preferred to stay with him because I loved him and felt he returned my affection. I simply couldn't work out what had happened to him, but, after a violent struggle, I managed to convince myself that it would be disloyal to leave his room now that he was so ill, even if he wanted me to.

After a while I approached him. The blanket over his head must almost have been stifling him; I'd never known him cover himself up like this, however cold it got in winter, or however many mosquitoes there were in summer.

I went up, thinking to touch him gently with my right hand, but decided, on second thoughts, that it would be better to call to him first. He didn't answer, but I could hear his muffled breathing and knew he wasn't asleep. I laid my hand on his shoulder.

"What's the matter with you tonight?" I said.

He didn't answer, and I repeated the question, pressing more firmly on his shoulder. A choking voice came out from beneath the blanket:

"Let me sleep!"

"Did I wake you?"

Without a word he turned towards the wall, and I could hear stifled sobs now.

Forcing myself to stay calm, I bent over him to find out what was wrong, but he wouldn't respond. Then, as I moved my hand from his shoulder onto his face, I found his face was soaked with the tears he was shedding. Deeply moved, I hastily drew my hand back.

That night was a very troubled one.

"My dearest brother," I said, "my faithful friend and only companion here in this room, please say something to me!"

When he didn't answer, I repeated this. At last he said:

"Leave me alone!"

"Do you want me to take my things and go away?" I said.

"Do what you like. You're free to choose."

"I've never been free—not since I was taken to the hostage fortress, and then brought to the palace of our Lord and Master the Governor, and Sharifa Hafsa's house!"

Again he made no reply, and I repeated my question, feeling now that I really should leave.

"Do what you like," he said again. "Leave me alone. I'm sick!"

"I'm worried about your illness."

"Don't bother your head about it."

"Do you want me to find somewhere else to sleep tonight?" I said, after a moment's silence. "Till you've calmed down and stopped acting like this?"

"I couldn't care less what you do."

I paused for a moment, deeply worried. Then I said:

"I want to know exactly how you feel about it."

"I'm sick and I want to rest—for ever."

"Please be frank with me."

"All right. Please find somewhere else to sleep, so I won't bother you with my illness."

"Have I ever complained?"

"Maybe you put up with more than you should have done."

"But you put up with me right from the start."

"That's silly, emotional talk."

"It's true, though."

"Leave me alone, please!"

"While you're like this?"

"Yes, I'll feel easier if I'm left alone here."

"But the women don't worry us any more now."

"That's not true. You and the Governor may be convinced of it—as the Governor and I were once. And yet we've still been doing the same kinds of thing. Haven't you noticed?"

"No."

"I'm older than you are."

"I'm not sure you are."

"Yes, I am. And when I came of age, became a young man, I tried to free myself from all these things I was doing. But I carried on, unfortunately, and just behaved like a stupid child."

There was no room left for argument, and I picked up my things and went out into the courtyard, rather uncertain where to go at that time of night. I walked, automatically, towards the *bourezan*'s lodgings, and found him outside his room looking out over the outer walls and whistling the tunes of some of the folk songs you hear at harvest time in my part of the country.

He welcomed me warmly, as if I was a close friend come to visit him. Why I went to him I don't know, because everyone said how reserved he was, and how he had no time for anyone, however high their position. He put my mattress down in a splendid spot in the round-shaped room, and, knowing how much store he set by seeing everything clean and tidy and in its proper place, I made the spot where I slept even neater than his own was.

One evening, as I was reflecting on the condition of my friend the *duwaydar*, the *bourezan* started telling me about his life and the things he'd done.

"Have you heard about the Great Retreat?" he asked me.

"Yes," I answered, "my father told me about it. When he was a young man he fought in the war that led up to it, along with my grandfather, who always rode on a mare."

"They attacked us from the edge of Tihama with their German-made guns. They were Wahhabis and Saayda, and we were Yemenis, both Sunni and Zuyud, with French rifles and bullets."[19]

My father had told us about some of these things, describing them down to the last detail.

"We were defeated," my friend the *bourezan* went on, "and we fell back from Tihama. When the peace treaty was made, we were crowded onto a small ship which took us back to Aden."

He continued to reminisce on his past glories.

"I learned to play the bugle from our old Turkish teacher, who stayed behind with the Turks that were left after their defeat. And so I became a *bourezan*."

"That's marvelous," I said.

"Your mind's somewhere else," he said. "What are you thinking about?"

I was embarrassed by the sudden question.

"Nothing at all," I said. "I'm fascinated by what you're saying."

"No you're not. There's something on your mind."

"Perhaps. I'm sorry."

"Is it Sharifa Hafsa?"

"I'd forgotten all about her."

"Then what's worrying you so much you look as if you were a hundred miles away?"

"My friend, the *duwaydar*."

"The handsome *duwaydar*?"

"Yes."

"Poor lad. He's naive, but he's good-hearted too."

"He's very sick. It's got to a critical point now."

"I'm very sorry to hear it. Even so, it wasn't very

---

[19] See note 12 above.

comradely of him to throw you out of his room."

"He had his reasons for it. But I should have stayed close to him even so, especially when he was so sick."

"Shall we go and see how he is?"

"That's what I wanted to ask you, but I was afraid of imposing on you."

*   *   *

Together with the *bourezan*, I visited my friend, the handsome *duwaydar*, where he lay sick in his small room. He was still in his bed, which he obviously hadn't left since my departure. The food in front of him was untouched, and there was an acrid smell. I opened the small window, whose faint light I always used to enjoy as it came through the pitch blackness of the room.

He woke as he sensed our entrance, but said nothing, and I wondered if he was now incapable even of speech. I was determined, as we left, that I must go back to stay in his room, and I went to the *bourezan*'s room to collect my things. When I'd returned I arranged my place as usual, wondering how on earth I could summon up the resources of patience and endurance to deal with the trial that lay ahead of me.

I exchanged a few words with him, and he became less tense and started speaking as if nothing had ever happened. I managed to get him to eat some of the food in front of him, then massaged his cold feet, arranged his bed and helped him to the bathroom to relieve himself.

His eyes began to shine, now, with energy and vitality. He was happy I'd come back, and, hard though he struggled to preserve an appearance of pride, it was as though life had returned to him.

Despite all these preoccupations I had, the image of Sharifa Hafsa would never leave my mind, awake or asleep. Her husky voice rang in my ears, constantly, urging me to become a man, and I could still feel the pain in my back, in the place where she'd hurled the stone. I imagined her standing and defending me to her brother, weeping with a sound that kindled the fire of cruel love inside me.

But I took every care of my friend in spite of this, and despite the many duties I also had in the Governor's reception room in the afternoons and evenings. The daily gatherings there were full of anxiety now, as if everyone was expecting some major upheaval. The coughing of my friend the *duwaydar* grew worse night by night, even though he simply stayed resting in his bed, while my other friend, the *bourezan* who'd been one of the heroes of the Retreat, sang constant patriotic songs about attacking the enemy and gaining the victory, even though no victory had ever happened! As for the old *tabashi*, whose head was permanently scarred from the wound the mule Zaafarana had given him, he continued to hum the folk songs he loved.

As for me, I couldn't forget the song the soldiers sang whenever they saw me:

Your mother, oh *duwaydar*, is distracted by her loss;
Her tears fall like rain . . .

I remembered my mother who'd fled with me from the guards of the Crown Prince, Sayf al-Islam, through the plantations of corn and sugar-cane, fearing I'd be kid-napped and taken hostage. For all her efforts, I'd been torn from her arms with a cruelty she hadn't known before, and made to ride to the city on a bumpy horse that had belonged to my father and his family.

*　　*　　*

One day, by some chance, I met her! A deep quiver passed through me, as though I were in the grip of some burning fever, the sweat poured from my brow and my mouth became dry.

"God be praised!" she said, as I tried to hurry quietly on. "I thought you'd gone away!"

"I meant to," I said.

"Where were you going?"

"Back home, to my own part of the country."

"That's odd! I didn't think a hostage was allowed back to his family till another one could be sent in his place."

I made no answer to this.

"You're an important hostage too. And my personal *duwaydar*—before the Governor got hold of you."

"He ordered me to stay with him."

"And said you were a man now, that you'd come of age!"

"You said that before he did."

"And so you changed from a handsome *duwaydar* to a dutiful servant. You wash the spitpots, and arrange the *nargilas*, and sweep the place out, and do all sorts of other things as well."

I said nothing.

"Is that what you call rising in life?" she went on.

125

Fleeing from her wounding sarcasm, which tore me to the very depths, I rushed to the main gate and—as if she was chasing me—took shelter from her with my friend the *bourezan*. I tried to hide my great agitation, afraid that it might burst out, but my kindly friend took me by the shoulders and shook me violently.

"What's the matter with you, you fool?" he said.

When I didn't answer, he gripped me still more powerfully.

"You're your mother's son!" he said.

I remembered my mother and the song the soldiers always sang:

Your mother, oh *duwaydar*, is distracted by her loss;
Her tears fall like rain . . .

I took a grip of myself.

"Has something happened to your friend?" he asked.

"No."

"What's the matter with you then?"

"Nothing."

"Nothing! You were crying like a little spoiled child!"

"I wasn't crying. When have you ever seen me cry?"

"If you won't tell me what the matter is, then by God . . ."

He left the sentence unfinished, and I said nothing either. He reflected for a moment.

"Is it Sharifa Hafsa again?"

I nodded.

"My poor hostage friend!" he said. "You'll either have to die for love of her, or run away from it all!"

"I'll run away!"

"What did she do to you, my poor young man?"

"Nothing."

"What did she say?"

"Words. Just words."

"Harsh words?"

I nodded.

"She taunted you, did she, with becoming the Governor's servant?"

I nodded again.

"And said you were stupid, and a coward, and you'd never be a man?"

I said nothing.

"Do you really love her?" he asked gently.

I hesitated.

"What a disaster for you!" he said.

I plucked up the courage to answer.

"Is love such a terrible disaster?" I said.

"Yes, it is such a terrible disaster—especially if it's returned by Sharifa Hafsa!"

*   *   *

That night, after carefully arranging the bed of my sick friend, the *duwaydar*, and getting him everything he needed, I lay awake all night long, because I'd drunk some wine to try and forget Sharifa Hafsa. I couldn't get her out of my mind for an instant. What was she doing at that moment? Was she lying in her soft bed, in all the beauty of her plump young body, her charms revealed clearly through her transparent clothes? I could hear her husky voice, filling my ears like the hissing of a snake!

From time to time my friend would sleep for a few

minutes between his fits of coughing, and I'd take advantage of this to drink another glass of wine and smoke another of his famous cigarettes.

The wine made me feel I was in a different world, and, without thinking too clearly about it, I decided to go to Sharifa Hafsa's house. Drinking another glass of wine, I went out into the courtyard, walked up to the house and knocked at the door. It was opened by a servant girl who knew me and let me in, and I climbed the stairs to Sharifa Hafsa's room. Then I stood at her door, hesitating. What could I possibly say to her at this time of night? Had she heard the knock at the door, and was she getting ready to see who it was coming so late to her house?

I decided to go back, and hurried towards the main door. Then, all at once, I heard her husky voice asking her servant who it was. The girl replied that it was the hostage.

I felt her breath suddenly caressing my neck.

"To what do I owe the privilege of this visit from the servant of our Master the Governor?"

I made no answer, wildly regretting my stupid adventure. She now stood completely facing me.

"What does the servant of my Master the Governor want from me?"

"Nothing," I replied—I had to say something!

She reacted wih astonishment.

"Nothing?"

"No, nothing."

"Then what exactly are you doing in my house?"

"I was looking for something I left here. But perhaps I'm wrong. I must have left it somewhere else."

"How very odd! Is it something that's important to you?"

128

"It used to be."

"How very odd! If it wasn't important, surely you could have waited till morning and let the servants help you find it?"

"I'm deeply sorry, Sharifa, for intruding. I'm very glad, at any rate, that I haven't disturbed your sleep."

"How polite you are! So very polite! But might not one of my servant girls have the thing you're looking for?"

"No."

"Do none of them appeal to you?"

I leapt angrily towards the door, but she took me by the shoulders and pulled me towards her till our bodies were pressed against one another, and I felt her panting. She kissed me till I felt ready to faint, then took me by the hand towards her favorite room. There she locked the door, then embraced me, and I melted beneath her second kiss, like molten metal in a goldsmith or black-smith's furnace.

I plucked the sweetest of kisses from her lips, and my hands wandered everywhere over the soft body I'd dreamed of for so long. Together we floated in pleasures till the roosters of morning crowed.

*   *   *

I started out of my sleep as my sick friend called out to know what had happened to me. I went to the small window where the dawn light was spreading.

"What's the matter with you?" he said. "Are you sick?"

"No, not at all. How are you feeling?"

"Much as usual, but I was worried about you."

"Why? What did you think had happened to me?"

"I thought you weren't well."

I'd been waking up late for the past few days, because my work in the Governor's reception room began in the afternoon and went on until midnight.

The health of my friend, the handsome *duwaydar*, had grown so much worse that he was almost like a skeleton. His skin had become pale, and he very rarely left his room; I'd bring him in all his meals, although he'd eat almost nothing, and then only at my insistence. He looked depressed and in constant pain, and things were made worse by his unhappy sense that the people living in the palace were neglecting him.

"No one's been to visit me," he told me once.

"They're all very busy," I said, "and you're not in such a bad state as all that."

He sighed, and was silent for a moment.

"And yet," he said, "so many of them came to see you when you were dangerously sick. But you don't remember that any more."

*　　*　　*

Still I scrupulously obeyed the Governor's order that I should always stay with him, preparing the reception room and looking after it during the gatherings, and keeping away from the parts where the women of the palace lived. Yet I'd be consumed with longing as I sat huddled by that small, lonely window in our room, and a small gray sparrow would shake its tail over the sill and remind me how she was my cool and tender refuge.

"It's been so long," I'd think, "since that bewitching husky voice of yours sounded in my ears. How lovely it is!

Long ago, in my own wonderful part of the country I've so often told you of, they seized me, and made a hostage of me, and a *duwaydar* in your palace, and a servant in the reception room of your brother, the honored Governor. And yet it's as if your lovely voice flows sweetly through all this, turning the harsh sounds ringing in my ears to an enchanting melody."

*   *   *

While I was preparing the Governor's reception room, I'd play records on the ebony gramophone which was always used so discreetly,[20] listening to Yemeni singers like Antari, Almaz and Qutabi. I'd stand aghast—yet laughing, too, at my feelings—as the voice of the singer, and his amazing lute-playing, emerged from that wooden box with the black record in it. The music stirred my imagination all the more for the miraculous way it came. All I could remember from the days when I was a child at home was the voice of our precious cow lowing for its food!

Then, when I'd finished getting the reception room ready, I'd close the gramophone, knowing I'd hear it again during the gathering, and even, perhaps, as so often happened, see real musicians performing, and a dancer too.

And yet still longing would take hold of me whenever I sat huddled by that small, lonely window in the room of my friend, the sick handsome *duwaydar*. I'd think of Sharifa Hafsa and imagine I was speaking to her.

---

[20] The author is probably implying that gramophones were initially regarded with suspicion by devout Muslims.

"A dove will coo, perhaps,"[21] I'd say, "or a sparrow will chirp, to remind me that you alone are my cool and tender refuge. How long it is, my own, beloved Sharifa with the husky voice, since that bewitching voice of yours sounded in my ears! Long ago, in my own wonderful part of the country I've so often told you of, they seized me, and made a hostage of me, and a *duwaydar* in your palace. And yet, it's as if your lovely voice flows sweetly through all this, turning the harsh sounds ringing in my ears to an enchanting melody."

*   *   *

I longed to see Sharifa Hafsa, even from a distance; and I'd steal a few minutes to watch her door, hoping to see her emerge, or gaze at her windows in the hope of catching a glimpse of her. I'd go too, with the utmost caution, to places where she often went herself, finding flimsy excuses if anyone asked me what I was doing there. One day I almost took the greatest risk of all by venturing out to the house of the handsome poet right outside the city, in the hope of seeing her go into his house, or leave it. But I wasn't able to slip away.

*   *   *

It wasn't till I met Sharifa Hafsa and fell under her spell that I ever willingly practiced the rituals of prayer.

There was a small mosque near the gate, topped by a white dome, an ancient mosque built as a tomb for some former venerated saints and looked after by the old

---

[21] In Arabic poetry the dove is a traditional symbol of nostalgic separation and a reminder of the distant beloved.

tabashi whose head had been battered by Zaafarana. Because the mosque was near his palace, it was the Governor himself who paid for the nightly oil lamp whose smoke would rise up into the oval-shaped ceiling, and he also gave the old *tabashi* a sack of grain every month for the work he did there.

I'd go and pray repeatedly in this mosque, late at night or at any other time of prayer, begging God to cure me of my love for Sharifa Hafsa and grant calm forgetfulness to my soul. I'd kneel there with the greatest reverence, and when I left I'd be filled with hope that God would answer my heartfelt prayers.

I'd be ashamed, sometimes, of behaving in this way— and it was all quite useless too, for the moment I went back through the palace gate, my eyes would wander to her house. Sometimes I'd even go and sit in front of it, in the hope of seeing her shadow as she passed.

*   *   *

When the uselessness of going to pray was finally borne in on me, I searched for some other way of forgetting her. Oh, God, I'd think, didn't You create anyone but her!

I flung myself into my work, and also spent a good deal of time looking after my sick friend, and sitting with the *bourezan* listening to his stories about the war in which he'd been defeated, and listening to the guards' ritual song. But still I couldn't forget her. I kept thinking about what she'd said, that I wasn't a *duwaydar* any longer, but a servant washing the spitpots, and gathering burning embers for the *nargilas*, and sweeping out the reception room at the end of the night.

*   *   *

Late one night I went back to my sick friend's room and threw myself down by the small window, with depression and frustration gnawing at my heart, utterly weary of life. I heard his coughs, mingled, now, with a groaning which was new. When I went over to him, he was quite still except for some slow movements of the head. His body was cold, his face deadly pale.

*   *   *

There was only one foreign doctor in the city, and perhaps in the whole country.

"There's nothing to worry about," he said in his broken Arabic. "One pill after every meal, and, God willing, all will be well. But he must come and see me again."

I fetched my friend out of the surgery, and the doctor went straight down to look at his rabbits. The smell of their dung filled me with longing; it recalled my home and my village, the smell of our ox and cow and sheep!

I tried to cheer my friend up by imitating the doctor's broken Arabic, but he just gave a faint smile. He was sick and getting worse every day, and the doctor's pills did no good at all.

*   *   *

I took him back to the doctor several times. And again and again I heard the same broken Arabic and was given the same pill which was his only remedy for the sick.

One morning, when I was alone, I tried to sing one of the folk songs from my village, but I couldn't manage it, and I couldn't whistle the tune either. Somehow I felt no joy now even from the dawning of a new day.

*   *   *

The atmosphere of the Governor's gathering was tense that day. The Governor himself seemed anxious as he wandered constantly in and out of the reception room, and the other regular guests were in a similar state. Everyone was so disturbed it was clear to me there was something wrong, that something had been happening or was going to happen.

One of the Governor's closest friends checked to see exactly who was there, then said:

"What's happened in Sanaa?"

"The Imam's been assassinated," the Governor said.

"Who was responsible?"

"The Liberals. The Constitutionalists."

There was complete silence for a while.

"Has Sayf left the city?" one of the Governor's relatives asked him finally.

"Yes."

"How did he manage it?"

"I don't know."

"Didn't he leave word with you?"

"He doesn't trust anyone."

I was stunned at these words, to which the whole gathering was now reacting.

The guests left earlier than usual, and the Governor disappeared into his palace. I went back and told the news to my friend, who sprang suddenly from his bed.

"The Imam's dead?" he cried.

"So I've heard."

He lay down again, and spoke more quietly now.

"Are you sure of it?"

"It's what I've heard."

He got up again.

"And Crown Prince Sayf, where's he?"

"He's left the city."

Again he lay back.

"They've done it all wrong," he said, as if talking to himself. "They should have dealt with Sayf al-Islam first!"

"What was that?"

"Nothing."

"Are you feeling all right?"

"I was!"

*   *   *

Does this *duwaydar* friend of mine, I thought, know so much more about things than I do? And he a sick man too, perhaps even dying? I wondered at this, and blamed myself as well, because I had more reason to be on the alert than he had.

I threw myself down on my bed, consumed with anxiety. The old Imam had been killed in Sanaa, and the Crown Prince had fled the city!

What would happen to my own family? Some of them were in hiding, others in prison, or else in exile. And I was a hostage and *duwaydar*, or rather a mere servant now, just because my father opposed the Imam's policy.

136

But the important thing was that the Imam was dead, and, still more important, slain by Yemeni hands. That much was certain. Even so, the tyrannical Crown Prince had managed to flee; that was a bitter blow.

*   *   *

The annals of our Yemeni people show that they're capable of doing anything if the desire for it once takes hold of their minds. They'll do it in a haphazard way sometimes, perhaps, but do it they will; and this, whatever people may say, is a great quality. Even if it needs all the patience and all the famous brooding resentment of camels, they'll finally hack the oppressor down!

*   *   *

To the Governor's surprise, I prepared the reception room early. I said nothing to him of my feelings about what had happened, nor did he ask me, or, indeed, say anything to me at all. He was a mean-spirited, malicious man, and I noticed, as I worked with him, how he'd express things to people that he didn't really feel. This was something I first learned from him, then applied to my own dealings with him, hateful though I found him.

*   *   *

I was eager to hear any news I could about what was happening, but they didn't speak of important matters that day. It was a silent gathering, rather, in which I sensed terror and anxiety. Something more, I thought, must certainly have happened; and these people's faces reflected the worry that I was living with too.

*　　*　　*

I got up earlier than usual, and wandered aimlessly about the palace and the surrounding buildings, even passing in front of Sharifa Hafsa's house. Was she anxious about what was happening, I wondered, or was all her interest focused on herself, and the poet, and perhaps on me?

*　　*　　*

The citizens of the Governor's province around the city, together with his tenant farmers and a few general supporters, started coming to the palace. Some of them had rifles slung, apparently casually, over their shoulders, while others leaned on staffs and hatchets. They'd sing at the gates of the palace:

Oh tree in leaf, so green,
God water you with His rain!

There was a whole throng of people, surging about everywhere, croaking out inappropriate things which irritated the Governor—even though he'd sent messengers to them himself, summoning them to honor him at this time of crisis; he'd sensed that resolution and firmness were required, together with a demonstration of strength from as many followers as possible.

Things went, in fact, as the Governor wanted them to, and people began to think he was going to resolve things in accordance with his own interests, some suggesting he would side with Sayf, others that he would support the Liberal Party. He was clearly happy with these conflicting rumors, which he encouraged to develop and spread.

* * *

I told my sick friend about all this.

"The Governor?" he said. "He's more royalist than the Imam himself!"

"How stupid I am!"

"You're just a child."

"I've been called that before."

"You mean by Sharifa Hafsa?"

"Yes, and by the *bourezan* too!"

He coughed suddenly—a hacking cough which didn't stop till I'd pressed his chest hard against my own. Then he said quietly:

"The *bourezan*? All he can talk about is the war where he was defeated. He goes on and on about it."

Perhaps my friend meant to change the subject by going off at a tangent like this. But I persisted.

"That isn't what I meant," I said.

"Well, you'll know about it in time anyway," he said.

Feeling that he was embarrassed, I didn't tell him the *bourezan* had once made much the same remark to me. We lay there, motionless, with just a flicker of light coming in through the small window, and his hacking cough never stopped except when I pressed him to my chest.

* * *

It was some time now since I'd heard that lovely, bewitching voice of hers. I'd told her how, in my own wonderful part of the country, they'd come and attacked me and my family, seizing everything and making a hostage of me, then a *duwaydar* in her palace and the servant of her brother, the Governor.

And yet her lovely voice kept flowing sweetly through all this, turning its harsh sounds to an enchanting melody.

*   *   *

It was by the fountain in the middle of the courtyard that I met her, as I was coming from the Governor's reception room after re-arranging it as usual when the final guest had left.

"Well, God be praised!" she said coquettishly. "It's as if we were strangers!"

I made no answer, trying to hide my embarrassment, but she came up and took me by the arm.

"Be careful," she said. "I'm Sharifa Hafsa!"

"I know that well enough!"

"And you're a hostage."

"And a *duwaydar*."

"A handsome *duwaydar*."

"What of it?"

"And the servant of our Master the Governor, who . . ."

"Who washes the spitpots, and so on, and so on."

"Well, it's true, isn't it?"

"Of course it is."

"I thought you might deny it."

Somehow I plucked up the courage to stand facing her

quite undismayed, feeling prouder and stronger than I'd ever felt before. Then I walked straight past her towards the gate of the palace.

"Where do you think you're going?" she said.

"I've something to do."

"So suddenly!"

"What do you want?"

"To see you."

"As simple as that?"

She gave her usual frown, then spoke in her bewitching, husky voice:

"You're going to leave me all alone?"

I pretended to inspect the space all around her, as if we were in some desolate forest where she was afraid of wild beasts.

"You're in your own home," I said.

"Am I?"

I was silent for a moment, only too well aware how her powers of sarcasm surpassed mine. I tried to rouse her to anger.

"All you care about is yourself," I said.

"And the people I love."

"You're just saying that!"

"Isn't it true?"

"No."

"Are you really quite sure of that?"

I didn't answer. Keeping control of her temper, she tugged me by the hand to a corner of the courtyard and made me sit down next to her. Then, in a voice I hadn't heard before, in which defeat and a sense of betrayal were evident, she said:

"I want you to save me."

I was shocked by the earnest, desolate way she said this, not recognizing the weakness her voice now betrayed.

"Who's going to save me before that can happen?" I said gently. "And who'll save the country?"

"I have to think of myself. God will take care of the country."

"I don't follow you."

"Ha!"

"What do you mean?"

"Haven't you read any history books?"

"History books? Not a page. But my father was always reading them."

She had been ready to burst into tears, but now she laughed, then gaily embraced me. I allowed my head to nestle between her breasts that were so full of warmth, and of love and desire. She pushed me gently away.

"Will you save me from the plight I'm in?" she said.

I smiled again, struck with awe by this sudden request.

"Save you from what?" I said, after a long reflection.

"From this life I lead," she said immediately.

"The man who's down in the valley," I said, turning to the traditional country wisdom I knew so well, "wants to be up in the mountains. And the man who's up in the mountains wants to be down in the valley."

"That's just some stupid provincial proverb!"

"It's proven wisdom that's been handed down."

She was silent for a moment, which gave me the chance to assess the situation properly.

"We're here in the same place," she said at last, "whether you call it a mountain or a valley."

"No," I replied, "we're as different as a valley is from a mountain."

"You mean I'm the Governor's sister, and you're a *duwaydar*, and a hostage, and a . . ."

"That's one of the differences."

"What's the other difference?"

"Do we really have to go on with this stupid conversation?"

She jumped up angrily and went towards her house.

In the city and the villages round about, the torches on the roofs of the houses were celebrating a momentous event.

*   *   *

Despite all the people's prophecies, the new Imam, the former Crown Prince, Sayf al-Islam, had been victorious over the Liberals and the Constitutional revolutionaries, and the victory torches had been lit and raised high on the Governor's house and the surrounding houses. I'd refused point blank to mix the kerosene and ashes the torches were made from, or to light them in celebration of the new Imam's victory; but others were ready and willing to do the job.

Feeling weak and wretched, I lay down by my sick friend, who was groaning with a painful hissing sound. I went to the small window and saw the torches shining from every rooftop, filling our room with their pale light.

The new Imam had won the victory, and I knew beyond doubt that my father had been among those beheaded in the town of Hijja. Sayf al-Islam had followed this by declaring Sanaa an open city for his men to loot and kill and destroy as they wished.

*   *   *

My friend, the handsome *duwaydar*, was dead. As I looked at him, lying cold and motionless there, I felt utterly desolate.

I thought I'd be distracted with grief by his death, but in fact I found myself accepting it silently and calmly. I embraced him, then washed him with my own hands and stood looking at his naked body with its pale skin and its bones that jutted out like a skeleton. I wrapped him in a white shroud the *bourezan* had bought and anointed him with precious perfumes provided by Sharifa Hafsa, who'd been keeping them aside for other occasions. Then I placed twigs of basil and fragrant flowers between the folds of the shroud.

I went to look for the *bourezan*, hoping he'd open my eyes and help me weep; but he was depressed himself, and he'd fled, taking with him the memories of his old defeat, sunk in a sense of dejection and failure which the failure of the recent revolution had no doubt increased.

How I wished he was there with me, especially as he'd played his part by buying the shroud! I wanted him to share my worries and concerns, and take my mind off them with his stories of his old, failed war.

As for Sharifa Hafsa, she came to the funeral, looking very sorrowful, the smell of her expensive perfumes rising from the wooden coffin. The old *tabashi* came too.

The three of us were the main mourners. Most of the women from the palace and the surrounding buildings, who'd known him from their adventures with him, looked on from afar.

It was a small funeral. We walked, with my friend's

coffin carried on our shoulders, to the city graveyard, now thronged with so many other funerals with their mournful chants:

There is no God but God, there is none but God,
None but God, and Muhammad is His prophet.

*   *   *

Your mother, oh *duwaydar*, is distracted by her loss;
Her tears fall like rain . . .
Your mother, oh *duwaydar*, is distracted by her loss;
Her tears fall like rain . . .

*   *   *

Oh God, we seek Your blessing.
Oh God, we seek Your blessing.
Oh God, we seek Your blessing.
Bless us with Your favor.
Oh God, grant us Your favor!
Almighty Lord, we seek You,
You Who open Your doors to us.

*   *   *

The songs filled my ears with overwhelming force, as I struggled to pave the way for the funeral procession and the coffin, through the narrow gate of the city and up to the crowded graveyard; and dominating all the others could be heard the chants of the new Imam's soldiers:

Oh, Houban Valley,[22] open wide
To the army of our Master, and our Master's guns!

Heard, too, were their ringing cries:

Oh, our Masters, you are the lights of this land!

*   *   *

The old *tabashi* had prepared a small grave. Although the coffin and the body in it were so light, I felt as though my neck was going to break, and I was utterly worn out; I'd been walking, bent, at the front of the coffin all the way from the palace to the graveyard. Some passers-by had volunteered to take turns with the carrying to win favor from God, but this did nothing to help me, because I'd never left my place at the front of the coffin and the funeral. The sweat was pouring from me now, and my eyes were stinging from it.

As we placed the coffin in front of the small grave, to recite the usual Sura of Yasin over it, I saw Sharifa Hafsa and some other women from the palace sitting by some old graves. Somehow I recognized her straightaway, even though she was wearing her black cloak like all the other women. I made no attempt to look in her direction again.

We threw the earth over the grave and its contents, and placed a stone over it as a sign that a man and not a woman was buried there. Then I plucked a piece of green shrub, put it on the grave and poured water on it.

Sharifa Hafsa came and laid her hands on my shoulders.

---

[22] Houban Valley: A famous valley in Yemen.

"May God grant you patience," she said.

I didn't know the proper formal answer to this. All I could remember from my own days at home was that we'd go out of the village whenever there was a funeral, chanting dirges, then read the Sura of Yasin over the grave.

"Shall we go back now?" she asked.

"I want to sit here a little," I answered.

"Why?"

"I just want to, that's all."

"Don't get upset. We all feel sad about him."

"Not as much as I do."

"Don't let your feelings run away with you."

"Feelings! There's no room for feelings in this palace or any of the buildings round it!"

She smiled.

"Don't be so arrogant and rude," she said calmly.

"What do you mean?"

She patted my shoulder again, and continued to speak calmly.

"I don't mean anything. I just think we should go home and rest, and try to forget."

"Forget what?"

Her composure left her.

"Forget this person who's died!" she said, in a shrill voice. "It's all over now!"

"I'll never forget him."

"None of us will ever forget him, but is that any reason for standing here all alone in a graveyard?"

Looking round, I saw there was no one but her, standing there in front of me; the overwhelming silence of the graveyard was all around us. But she sat down on a stone, and I sat down by her side.

We hadn't, I knew, found any solution to our problem.

I sat thinking over different plans I'd been forming ever since the victory torches had been lit for the new Imam. As for her, I don't know what she was thinking. I told her I'd only leave the graveyard when I felt like it.

"It's lunchtime," she said. "The Governor may need you."

I made a few rude, cutting remarks about the Governor and everyone else, but she kept her temper.

"Calm down!" she said.

"I'm not angry."

"Is there something wrong with you?"

"No."

"You're sad?"

"Perhaps."

* * *

We sat on there till nightfall.

"Have you any idea what we're going to do?" she said.

Silence enveloped the graveyard, as dusk, with its sad, unreal sun I so loved, began to fade and die. I wished all our life could be one unending twilight, where we dreamed like drunkards or smokers of hashish, floating, like them, in a world of the imagination, in the warmth that kindles the mind of those who chew *qat*.

"Yes," I said. "I have."

"You're going to run away?"

"Yes."

"You can't do that."

"Why not?"

She was silent for a moment, then spoke earnestly, and with fierce defiance:

"Because I won't leave you."

"I'll escape your clutches this time."

"You can't."

I contemplated her for a moment.

"It's just wishful thinking on your part," she went on. "You'll never be able to do it."

"No, I've made up my mind."

"Then I'll just have to throw stones at you till you bleed!"

"You can throw bombs at me if you like!" I said.

*   *   *

We were silent again, as the twilight departed and the gloomy night and the desolate silence of the graveyard sank down over us.

"Where will you go?" she said.

"To hell!"

"I'm trying to be serious. Why are you snapping back at me?"

"That's the way I am."

"It's not the way you are at all. You're handsome and sweet-natured."

"I used to be."

We fell silent again. Then she drew nearer to me, nearer than she'd ever come at any time before, and I felt her plump, soft body enfolding me in all its warmth. Her sweet lips, as she spoke, were moving close to my face, and her eyes, whose gaze I'd avoided for so long, were fixed on mine.

I couldn't return her gaze, nor could I make any answering reaction to her nearness. Perhaps I was afraid, or struck with awe.

149

It was pitch black all around us now. She took me by the shoulders to try and force me to face her, then spoke in a firm voice:

"Take me with you."

"Where?"

"To hell."

"Which hell?"

"The one you're going to."

I was terrified, hearing that beloved, husky voice say these things in such an utterly serious way.

"Sharifa . . ." I said earnestly.

"Don't call me that!"

"My darling . . ."

"Be a man. Make up your mind how you want to be."

"How do you want me to be?"

"Do you love me?"

"Yes."

"And do you believe I love you? Do you really believe it?"

"I'm not always really sure of it."

"I told you, be a man!"

"You've talked like that before! You don't really mean it!"

"It's not just idle talk now."

"It is. I know who it is you love, and I know how ambitious you are."

"You're talking about ambitions again!"

"I'm talking about truth—the truth you can't escape from!"

"The truth is that you don't understand."

"The truth is that you're ambitious, and you don't know how to love."

She calmed down a little.

"I said I want you to take me with you."

"That's ridiculous!"

"You're a coward."

"You may think so."

Again she controlled herself, and made a show of arranging her clothes. Then she turned to me and said:

"I'm not leaving you."

"You'll have to whether you want to or not," I said.

She leapt to her feet and picked up a stone to hurl at me, but I'd already started running. Stones kept falling all around me, but, for all my compassion for her, I didn't stop.

Still her beloved, husky voice rose, piercing my ears; in front of me was the darkness of the mountains, overlooking the desolate valley that descended, with me, towards an unknown future. I expected all the time to hear her voice or feel a stone striking my back, but already I'd gone a good way down this new road leading to my future life, leaving behind her beloved voice, and the memories of my dead friend, and of the *bourezan*, and the *tabashi* who'd been kicked by the mule, and his colleagues, the guards, with their everlasting chant:

Your mother, oh *duwaydar*, is distracted by her loss;
Her tears fall like rain . . .

About the Translators

May Jayyusi was born in Amman, Jordan to Palestinian parents, and was educated at London University and Boston University. She is a PROTA reader and translator, and has worked extensively in the process of selection of the poetry and fiction translated by PROTA. Aside from her work on PROTA's four anthologies of Arabic fiction and poetry, she has translated Ghassan Kanafani's *All That's Left to You and Other Stories* (1990), and Ibrahim Nasrallah's acclaimed *Prairies of Fever* (1993). She has also translated a collection of the poetry of Muhammad al-Maghut, *The Fan of Swords* (1991) and is presently working on the translation of Yahya Yakhlif's novel *The Lake*. She lives with her husband and two children in Jerusalem.

Christopher Tingley was born in Brighton, England, and was educated at the universities of London and Leeds. Following initial teaching experience in Germany and Britain, he lectured in the fields of English Language and Linguistics at the University of Constantine, Algeria, the University of Ghana, the National University of Rwanda and the University of Ouagadougou, Burkina Faso. In the field of translation, he collaborated with the author on the translation of the extracts of Arabic poetry in S. K. Jayyusi's two volume work *Trends and Movements in Modern Arabic Poetry*; for PROTA, he has co-translated (with Olive and Lorne Kenny as first translators) Yusuf al-Qa'id's novel, *War in the Land of Egypt* (1986), Liyana Badr's *A Balcony over the Fakihani* (1993), with Peter Clark as first translator, and many short stories.